Readers love ANDREW (

Range… novels

GW00758840

A Shared Range

"…This is one of those stories to read when your heart is bruised and your world feels dark. You'll take a deep breath afterwards and see the sun again."

—Whipped Cream Reviews

"It's another enjoyable read filled with two well rounded and likable guys in Dakota and Wally, a great premise, a beautifully described mountain locale and two fun and interesting supporting characters in Phillip and Mario."

—Literary Nymphs

A Troubled Range

"This is one book that I won't forget and you shouldn't miss it."

—Fallen Angel Reviews

"*A Troubled Range* is more than two people finding love but also about family secrets coming out in the open, acceptance of one's self and finding that love is not something you look for but one worth fighting for."

—Love Romances and More

"…it's sweet, a little sad, and the scenes and people come alive for the reader."

—Night Owl Reviews

http://www.dreamspinnerpress.com

AN
UNSETTLED
Range

ANDREW GREY

Dreamspinner Press

Published by
Dreamspinner Press
4760 Preston Road
Suite 244-149
Frisco, TX 75034
http://www.dreamspinnerpress.com/

An Unsettled Range
Copyright © 2012 by Andrew Grey

Cover Art by Reese Dante   http://www.reesedante.com

ISBN: 978-1-61372-329-6

Printed in the United States of America
First Edition
January 2012

eBook edition available
eBook ISBN: 978-1-61372-330-2

To my brother, David.

Prologue

"ARE you still here?"

Troy Gardener looked up from his desk as Cameron Jarvis stood in his doorway, dressed in jeans and some fancy designer T-shirt. Troy checked the clock.

"I think the more important question is why *you're* here at this hour. You never work this late," Troy responded, narrowing his eyes suspiciously. They were both up for the same job as director of the Interior Department, and while Troy had always put in long hours, once the list of candidates had been announced, Cameron had started working later as well.

"I had some papers I wanted to review this weekend, and after taking Gail and the kids to Savage Mill for dinner, I stopped in to get them," Cameron said lightly with the easy smile he always seemed to have. The man was too annoying for words, with his designer jeans and shirts. Troy would never admit it to anyone, but Cameron was always just too comfortable in his own skin, and that irked Troy no end. He worked hard to fit in and to appear competent and knowledgeable, and for Cameron it always seemed to come so easily. "You have a great weekend, and tell Jeanie I said hello. And tell her Gail would love to get together with her again soon." Cameron hoisted the file in a farewell gesture. Even his own wife was cavorting with the enemy. Troy realized how stupid he was being the moment the idea crossed his mind. No matter who got the promotion, he'd still have to work with Cameron; he just hoped he'd be doing it as his boss. Troy returned the wave and went back to his work, finishing the task Cameron had interrupted before shutting down his laptop and removing it from its docking station and sliding it into his bag for the trip home. Troy then left his government office building and drove home.

It was summer, but the skies were already darkening as he pulled out of the parking lot and drove down the manicured, tree-lined driveway toward the street, the gate opening when the security guard recognized him. He returned the man's wave and began the drive home. Even though it was Friday, he'd still worked until almost nine o'clock. "I want that promotion to director," he'd explained to Jeanie that morning when she'd asked him to come home early. "It shouldn't be much longer," Troy had added, even though he really didn't know how long it would be before the head of the agency made his decision. Troy tightly gripped the wheel at the thought of that promotion going to Jarvis. Troy deserved it; hell, he wanted it more than the other man. Troy put the thoughts out of his mind the farther he got from the office and the closer he got to what he hoped would be a quiet weekend.

Jeanie had called a few hours ago to remind him that their daughter Sofia was at a sleepover at Callie's, and that she and her sister were taking their mother out for her birthday, so Troy was expecting a quiet evening at home by himself. He reached into his pocket for his smart phone before remembering that he'd forgotten it that morning. He'd done that all day, and it annoyed him no end that he'd left it at home; he sort of felt naked without it.

Turning onto his quiet street, he expected the house to be dark. Instead, he saw lights on, and when he turned into the driveway, there was a car he didn't immediately recognize parked in the driveway. "Damn it," he swore softly as he recognized it as his brother's. He'd forgotten that Kevin was spending the night at the house. Parking behind his brother, Troy grabbed his bag off the passenger seat and closed the door behind him before striding up the walk and climbing the stairs to the porch.

Troy couldn't help stopping to look around. He and Jeanie had admired this particular house for years, an original Queen Anne Victorian with a round turret and plenty of character. When the house had come on the market two years ago, they'd put in an offer right away, and Jeanie had spent every spare minute working on it once it was theirs. Troy's wife was amazing—she could do just about anything, and Troy had seen the house transform from a rough building into a home. He'd helped as well, because he hadn't been working the long hours then, but once the house was done, Troy had found the time he spent at work growing more and more.

"Hi, Troy."

His brother's voice pulled him out of his thoughts, and Troy saw Kevin stand up from where he'd been sitting in one of the porch chairs. "Jeanie asked me to tell you that she has some chicken salad for you in the refrigerator."

"Thanks," Troy answered before going inside. He set his bag next to the table in the hallway before walking up the stairs to his and Jeanie's bedroom. Pulling off his work clothes, he placed them with the other dry cleaning before pulling on a comfortable pair of jeans and a shirt. Stepping back down the stairs, Troy heard his phone vibrate, telling him that he had a text, and he scooped it up off the hall table, shoving it into his pocket, knowing he'd read the message later.

Kevin followed him into the kitchen, and Troy opened the refrigerator door, pulling out the plate Jeanie had set up for him, and while he was at it, he pulled out two beers as well. Troy didn't say anything as he handed Kevin a beer and walked out to the front porch, where he sank into one of the chairs. "What time is your flight in the morning?" Troy held the plate and began to eat. Jeanie was an amazing cook, and the food tasted wonderful.

"Eight o'clock. This is a long one." Kevin settled in the chair, appearing slightly agitated about something.

"Where are you going?" Troy asked, more to be polite than out of curiosity.

"Australia for two weeks. Peter wishes he could go with me, but he can't get the time off work." Peter was Kevin's partner of almost ten years now. They'd had their commitment ceremony two months before he and Jeanie had gotten married.

"That's too bad," Troy said, returning his attention to his plate, and he heard Kevin set his beer bottle on the porch ledge. Kevin didn't say anything, and Troy could feel his brother staring at him. His first instinct was to snap at him, but Troy held his tongue. He and Kevin had tentatively built a relationship as adults after years of avoiding each other after their teenage years where they had fought like cats and dogs. Troy knew he was probably largely to blame. He'd hated having a gay brother because of the way it reflected on him. And Kevin had never hidden who he was—he'd been out and proud since he was fifteen. "So work is going well?" Troy asked to break the silence.

"Yes. Too much travel lately, but I think that should change after this trip, and this winter Peter and I are taking a cruise to the Caribbean, just the two of us," Kevin answered before taking another swig of beer, and silence descended once more. Troy heard Kevin shifting nervously in his chair. Truthfully, Troy barely noticed it. Kevin had always been the nervous type, and Troy had used it to his advantage more than once when they were kids. Now he barely paid attention to it. Troy finished eating and set his plate on the small table next to his chair.

"Troy." Kevin caught his eye, and Troy saw him look around like he was making sure no one could hear. "I think it's time we cut the crap." Troy glared at his brother. "You left your phone at home, and it kept beeping, so I switched it to vibrate. I saw your text messages."

Troy jumped to his feet, standing over Kevin. "What the hell were you doing looking at anything in my house!" Troy knew he could always intimidate Kevin, but this time Kevin stared back at him levelly, almost calmly.

"Like I said, cut the shit, Troy. I saw your texts. I know the kind of messages you're getting from Harry." Kevin kept his voice low, which unnerved Troy even more. "What is it you're playing at?"

Troy picked up his plate and left the porch without saying a word, walking into the kitchen to put it in the sink. "You had no right."

Kevin lightly touched his shoulder with one hand. "Does Jeanie know?"

Troy couldn't move or breathe as he stared into the sink. He expected to blink and wake up at any minute from this nightmare. But he didn't—this was real. Troy shook his head once before shrugging off his brother's touch and walking into the family room. He didn't have to look to know that Kevin had followed right behind him. Troy turned on the television before glaring at his brother, daring him to say another word. But for once it didn't seem as though it was going to work.

"Talk to me, Troy. I've known you longer than any other person on earth, and I most certainly know what you're feeling." Kevin sounded so understanding, but Troy didn't want to talk about this, not in the least. All he wanted to do was get Kevin to shut up about it so he could go back to his life the way it was. "Troy, is this why you've been working yourself to the bone? You're never home; I know that. You and Jeanie rarely take vacations together, and when you do, it's always with a group of people. The two of you are never together anymore."

"I do not want to talk about it!" Troy ground out between clenched teeth.

"I don't really give a crap right now," Kevin told him firmly. "You need to deal with this. You have a wife and a child, and you're getting texts from some guy about meeting you at a gay bar." The excuse, the cover story, was right on the tip of his tongue, but Kevin cut him off. "We aren't teenagers, and this isn't you getting drunk and covering it by saying you ate bad pizza. This is your life and your peace of mind."

"Then leave me alone," Troy said.

"I can't. There's more than your happiness at stake. What about Jeanie and Sofia? You aren't doing them any favors sneaking around behind their backs. Let me help you."

"I don't need your help," Troy countered feebly. He'd wished these feelings away for years, and he'd stayed far away from anything and anyone who might interfere with his life, the life he'd built with his wife and child. Troy had supported his brother once they were no longer teenagers. He and Jeanie had attended his brother's commitment ceremony and had helped with the arrangements. Troy was proud of his brother, and at the same time, he was as envious of him as he could possibly be.

Troy reached for the remote and turned up the volume. He knew if Kevin said anything, he would simply deny it and offer Jeanie an explanation and she'd accept it. He was sure of that. To calm his nerves, he tried to watch the television, but then it clicked off, and Kevin stared at him like he was a child dragged in front of the principal. Troy stared back, waiting to see what his brother would say, but Kevin remained quiet. Then Kevin sat next to him on the sofa and did something totally unexpected: he hugged him, tight. Troy began to struggle, but Kevin wasn't about to let him go. "I know what's in your heart, little brother. I know about your shame and how you cover up who you really are. It doesn't matter, because I love you no matter what."

Troy heard the hitch in Kevin's voice but did his best to ignore it. He was not going to let anyone get under his skin. He couldn't. "Kevin," he said forcefully, but his brother would not let go.

"I know you're gay, Troy, and I know you've resented me all these years. I came out and you hid. That's eaten at you for a long time, and you need to let it go and allow yourself to be who you are. Who you always were."

Troy stood up, shrugging away from Kevin. "Who I am is Jeanie's husband and Sofia's father. There's no way I can be gay."

Kevin sat back on the sofa, looking at him patiently. There had not been many times in his life that Kevin had managed to rattle him, but he was sure doing it now. "You are gay. It's just part of who you are, and the sooner you face it, the easier your life is going to be. You've been skirting the issue all your life, and you're still doing it now. I noticed that you didn't deny it—you just tried to deflect, but it won't work. So go on hiding if you want, but I know you for who you are, and you can't hide forever, no matter how hard you try. It'll eat at you from the inside, because every time you think about being with someone else for any reason, you know you're cheating on Jeanie."

"What in the hell am I supposed to do?" Troy asked, more loudly than he meant to, and he heard his voice crack as some of his willpower deserted him. "If you have all the answers, then what am I supposed to do so everyone doesn't get hurt?"

Kevin stood and placed his hand on Troy's shoulder, the warmth soaking through his clothes. "I don't have all the answers. I never did. And I don't see a way to keep people from getting hurt. When you've been hiding who you are for as long as you have, making a change is going to hurt people. And in this case, it's going to hurt the ones you love most. I know that. I will tell you this: you don't have to do anything right away. Think things through. You need to be honest with yourself about how you feel before you can be honest with anyone else." Troy saw his brother swallow hard. "But you know it doesn't matter to me. I'll love you no matter what." Kevin hugged him again, and this time Troy returned it. He could feel some of the walls, some of the barriers he'd spent a lifetime building, begin to crumble, and he held on to Kevin as the emotions he'd held at bay surged to the surface. As Kevin hugged him, Troy wiped his eyes, trying desperately to hold himself together.

The sound of a car door closing outside brought him back to reality, and Troy stepped away from Kevin, swallowing around the lump in his throat. Walking away, he went into the bathroom, running cold water and splashing it on his face before staring at himself in the mirror. Troy always thought he knew who was staring back at him from the mirror, but now as he stared, he saw a stranger. Everything he thought he knew about himself was wrong, and he wasn't sure if he could live with this image or not. Taking a deep breath, Troy steadied his nerves as he heard Jeanie saying hello to Kevin, and then their voices grew softer and faded away.

Clamping his eyes closed, Troy shut out the image from the mirror and tried his best to keep his emotions from bursting to the surface, but the genie had been let out of the bottle, and he couldn't shove those feelings back down. The images of the bathroom tile became watery as tears welled in his eyes. What in the hell was he going to do? The last thing he wanted was to hurt Jeanie and Sofia. They were his entire life.

Troy had been married before. His first wife, Mary, had been extremely career-oriented to the point that there was no way she ever wanted children. Troy had, and for that reason, as well as others, their marriage had eventually ended. Troy could always chalk the end of his first marriage up to differences that he and Mary could never work through, but now that he was facing some of the truth in his life, he wondered just how much Mary had known or sensed, because she had since remarried, and Troy had learned that she'd given birth to twins.

The truth of his life and the decisions he'd made began to hit him all at once, and Troy felt his knees begin to shake. Then he felt the floor coming up to meet him, and he offered no resistance as he crumpled onto Jeanie's pale yellow bathmat. Covering his eyes with his hands, Troy did his best not to make a sound as his mouth opened and he gasped for air, crying silently until parts of the mat felt as though he'd actually taken a shower. Troy had no idea what he was going to do, but no matter what he decided, the tears he was shedding were not going to be the last ones, that was pretty plain.

Forcing himself first to his knees and then to his feet, Troy stared into the mirror again as he heard a soft knock on the door. "Are you okay?" Kevin asked from the hallway.

"Yes," Troy answered softly, not really trusting his voice not to give him away. Turning on the water, he wiped his eyes with a cold cloth before flushing the toilet and then opening the door. Troy found Jeanie and Kevin on the porch enjoying the fresh summer evening, and all Troy could think about was the pain and heartache he was going to cause his family. And the biggest question on his mind as he sat and stared at the lightning bugs that lit the trees around the property was how easily he could end it all.

Chapter One

DAMN, his feet hurt, along with everything else. A car approached, and Liam stuck out his thumb, trying desperately to hitch a ride to anywhere, but the car continued on past, kicking up a cloud of dust that added another layer to what was already caked onto every inch of his skin. There was so much dirt on him it hurt to move his arms from the grit that had worked its way beneath them. It felt like weeks since he'd been clean, and even longer since his belly was full and he'd had a proper chance to sleep. He felt as though his eyes wanted to close on their own and like his legs were made of lead, but still he walked. Liam looked around for the millionth time, but all he saw was flat land and cattle. He knew that someone had to own the cattle and someone had to live around here, but he hadn't seen a house in forever. At the last one, some old guy had waved a gun at him.

The low rumble of another car caught Liam's attention, and he turned around, thumbing for a ride once again. This car looked fast, and Liam tried to appear hopeful. As the low red car approached, it veered toward him, and Liam stepped back, falling into a shallow ditch, landing hard on his ass as the car screamed by without the slightest sign of slowing down. Closing his gritty eyes, Liam took inventory and realized that at least nothing hurt more than it had before. He supposed he should feel lucky, but it was hard with your ass in a ditch and what little you had in the world strewn on the ground. Moving slowly, because it was all he could do, Liam gathered up his things, sticking them back into his pack. He clamped his eyes closed to stop the cry of frustration and maybe something else as he watched the last of his water leak out of his now cracked and useless water bottle. To make matters worse, the sun was setting, and Liam could already feel a slight chill in the air. He should be used to it by now, but he was so tired and hungry, his brain had stopped working well. Somehow, through sheer will, Liam got back to his feet and continued down the road, walking and shuffling as the sky continued to darken. He kept scanning around for lights that might denote a house or any kind of building, but he saw nothing.

Liam had long ago stopped swallowing because his throat felt like sandpaper. He was only adding more pain to what he was already feeling. It was now nearly pitch black, with only the stars providing any light at all. No cars had passed in hours, and Liam could feel his body giving up. Stumbling over nothing, he tumbled down by the side of the road and stayed there. He no longer had the energy to move or the strength to go on. Not that it mattered. No one wanted him around, and it would be easier if he simply lay down and died, which was sounding better and better all the time. Shrugging off his pack, Liam rested his head on it as the cold from the night, the hunger, the pain, and the tiredness that went to his bones all receded to nothing.

Voices pierced his peaceful dreams, and he thought they were part of it except they sounded urgent and his dream had been so pleasant and happy. "Be careful," someone scolded lightly.

"Is he dead?"

He felt someone touch his neck, warm and gentle. "No."

Liam wanted to move into that touch, but he couldn't seem to make anything work except his ears, so he let the dream continue. In the dream he was floating on clouds and then the clouds began to bump and jerk. Slowly, Liam's mind began to work, and he realized he wasn't dreaming. Opening his eyes was painful, but he saw jittering lights, and he realized he was in some sort of vehicle. He tried to move away so he could get out, but nothing seemed to work.

"It's okay. You're going to be all right, I promise. No one is going to hurt you."

Liam decided to take the voice at face value, not that he had a choice. Liam heard a rush of air and then the voice spoke again. "Mario, he's awake." Then the air stopped, and Liam let everything go. Whatever happened to him happened; he was way past caring.

"Drink slowly," the same voice said, and Liam did as he was told, cool water sliding down his throat. It hurt at first, but then it felt good, and he reached for the glass, but it slipped away. "Not too fast." Liam took another drink and more water slid down his throat and hit his empty stomach. He kept sipping until the glass slipped away from his lips. "You can have some more in a few minutes." Liam felt his body settle against something soft, and he was warm. He lost track of time.

"Drink a little more."

Liam complied, and this time, the water had flavor, and he drank and drank.

"What's in that?" another voice asked.

"Gatorade mixed with water. He probably hasn't had anything to eat in days, and he needs something simple to get his stomach working again." Liam opened his eyes and found he was in a dim room. There were two people staring back at him with worried looks on their faces. "Feeling better?" Liam nodded and took the glass, gulping from it before anyone could stop him. Then he coughed, and the man took the glass back. "You need to take it easy. You can have more when your stomach gets used to working again."

"Who are you?" Liam croaked, his throat hurting.

"I'm Wally, and this is Mario," the man answered. "We found you on the side of the road." Liam tried to sit up, and the man gently pressed him back down. "Take it easy. You're dehydrated, and we need to get fluids into you slowly. When was the last time you ate?"

Liam shrugged. He wished he could remember. "Couple of days, I guess. I'm Liam, Liam Southard," he added hastily, remembering his manners.

Wally handed the other man the glass. "Go ahead and fill it half and half with water and Gatorade."

Mario nodded and hurried away. "What were you doing out there at this time of night? We nearly didn't see you."

"Walking. Been trying to find work for weeks. Spent a day or so working on a ranch south of here, but they kicked me off and I moved on. Ain't had nothin' to eat since." Liam tried to turn away from Wally's concerned gaze. He didn't deserve that look. Mario returned with the glass, and Liam practically snatched it when it was offered, drinking as much as he could get.

"Hey. Take it easy. You can have more," Wally told him gently.

Liam drained the glass and then handed it back. "Thank you kindly." The much bigger man took the glass and left, returning with another that he set on the table. Liam relaxed for a second until he remembered his pack, looking frantically around him.

"Your pack is on the floor by the sofa. Rest awhile and don't drink too much all at once," Wally told him, and the two men left the room. Liam looked around and saw pictures on the walls of what was obviously a ranch house. He heard kitchen sounds, and his stomach rumbled loudly, reminding Liam forcefully that he hadn't eaten in days. Liam reached for the cup and took another drink. He was still thirsty, but the immediate compulsive need had been satisfied, and he sipped from the glass, waiting to see what would happen next. Wally came back into the room carrying a plate with two pieces of toast on it. He handed him the plate, and Liam took a bite before inhaling the rest of the food. "We'll let that settle, and then I'll get you something else."

Liam nodded and handed back the plate, his eyes drifting closed. "Thank you."

"Just relax. You're safe." He felt a warm hand touch his forehead and then move away. Liam's mind began to drift, and he heard people moving quietly around him, but he didn't open his eyes. If this was a dream, he didn't want to do anything to wake himself up.

Liam jumped at the snap of a door closing near him, and then he thumped onto the floor, staring up at the huge man who was staring back at him. Before Liam could speak, he heard footsteps hurry through the house. "Kota!" Wally cried and then launched himself into the big man's arms. Liam saw them hug, and then to his surprise the two men were kissing. Liam blinked a few times before climbing back onto the sofa, pulling his gaze away from the two men. Pulling up the blanket, he listened as Wally and this Kota person talked softly behind him, and Liam found himself thinking that he might have actually died and gone to heaven.

Liam stared at the ceiling and saw Kota's large frame looming over him. "Wally said you were really dehydrated. Are you injured anywhere else?" Kota knelt near the sofa and pulled away the blanket. Liam tried to hold it in place. "It's all right. I'm a doctor, and I just want to make sure you're not injured."

"I'm okay," Liam said nervously. "Maybe I should get out of your hair."

"You can go if you want. No one will stop you, but Wally said you haven't eaten much in days, so you have to be hungry. There's nothing to be afraid of," Kota said reassuringly, and Liam looked toward Wally, who nodded. "Do you think you can walk?"

Liam nodded and slowly got to his feet. He felt as weak as a baby, but managed to get his legs beneath him before following the two men into the kitchen. Liam pulled out a chair and sat down as Kota sat next to him. "How did you come to be lying in a ditch by the side of the road?"

"I've been looking for work," Liam answered honestly. "I come up this way from Texas to outside Pinedale because I had this job waitin' for me, and when I got there, the foreman hired me on like was promised, but after one day, the boss sees me and says he didn't want no fags on his ranch." Liam paused to swallow and catch his breath. "The foreman paid me for the day, and I found myself out of a job. I got there by bus and I didn't have the money for another ticket. I tried to get a job at one of the other ranches, but the boss had put the word out, and no one would hire me." Liam felt his upper lip begin to shake, and when Wally set a plate of scrambled eggs and toast in front of him, Liam fought to keep all the pain and fear he'd had heaped on him over the past few weeks from bursting to the surface. Lowering his head away from the kind looks he was getting from both men, Liam slowly began to eat.

"That's almost a hundred miles from here. Did you walk the entire way?" Kota asked.

Liam nodded as he kept eating, the food tasting unbelievably good. "I heard that there may be work up here, but no one would stop to give me a ride," Liam said around the food, unable to stop eating for anything. "I stopped at a few places, but they weren't hiring and sent me on my way." Liam continued eating, scraping the last of the food off the plate. Wally took his plate and brought back some more, and soon Liam was actually starting to feel full, a sensation he'd thought he might never feel again.

Wally took the plate from in front of him, placing it in the sink. "Kota, Liam is dead on his feet, and he needs to sleep. You can talk to him in the morning." Wally touched the other man on the shoulders, and Liam saw Kota lean into the touch. "I'll show you the guest room."

Liam nodded and stood up, retrieving his pack from near the sofa before following Wally down the hall. Liam nearly moaned out loud when he saw the double bed with its homemade quilt. "Is there a place I can clean up?"

"The bathroom's right across the hall. I'll set out some clean towels for you. Do you have fresh clothes to put on?"

Liam shook his head slowly, feeling embarrassed and ashamed.

"I'll bring you some and lay them on the bed. Don't you worry about it. Dakota's things may be a bit big for you, but they'll do for tonight. There's soap and shampoo in the shower, so help yourself." Wally hurried away, and Liam stared down at the inviting bed and then looked at himself in the mirror above the dresser. He gasped when he saw his own face: scruffy beard, drawn eyes and mouth, black bags beneath his eyes. His forehead was streaked with dirt, and his hands looked like he had a tan, but it was just layers of dust and dirt. Wally returned and placed some clothes on the edge of the bed before leaving again.

Liam set down his pack before walking across the hall to the bathroom. A new toothbrush and toothpaste, as well as a razor and shaving cream, sat on the counter. A drawer had been left open with travel-size everything inside. Liam slowly closed the bathroom door before leaning against the counter as tears welled in his eyes. These people didn't know him from Adam, and yet they were nicer to him than his own mama and daddy. He wasn't quite sure how to take that or understand it. What he did understand was that in the morning he was going to ask Dakota for a job and hope like hell they needed another hand. He'd seen Wally and Dakota together, so at least he knew they wouldn't be running him off for liking stallions instead of fillies. God, he hoped he could stay here, because if the rest of the people here were as nice as Wally, Dakota, and Mario, he knew this place was damned near heaven.

Pulling himself out of his hopes, Liam began the process of making himself look more human. After stripping out of his clothes, Liam started the shower, and when the water had warmed, he stepped under the spray and closed his eyes. Few things in his life had felt as glorious. Opening his eyes, Liam nearly jumped back when he saw the brown water swirling around his feet. It took him a few seconds before he realized all the dirt was coming off him. Reaching for the soap, Liam began washing every inch of his skin. He found a small nail brush in the corner of the tub and used it everywhere he possibly could.

After washing himself at least twice, Liam turned off the water and stepped out of the tub. The face that stared back at him now seemed more like himself, but he wasn't quite there yet. Liam shaved and then brushed his teeth. By the time he was done, he felt normal and human. Wrapping a towel around his waist, Liam cracked the door and stole across the hall into the room he'd been given to use. He pulled on the clothes Wally had left for him before returning to the bathroom, where he found Wally cleaning up and gathering his clothes. "I'd wash these for you, but I don't think they'll survive the machine. I'll try, though, and if you have anything else, I'll wash it as well."

"You don't have to do that," Liam said softly, but just the thought of being clean for a while was enough to make him smile.

"It's no problem," Wally said as he took the clothes that Liam pulled from his pack. "And if they don't survive, we can help you get new ones, so don't worry."

Liam nodded and stared at the other man. "Why are you doing this? Why are you helping me?"

Liam saw Wally's eyes widen. "Hasn't anyone ever helped you before?" Liam shook his head, and Wally tutted lightly. "Well, we're helping because it's the right thing to do. Now, why don't you get in bed and sleep? No one will get you up in the morning, so come on out when you wake up, and we'll get you fed." Wally smiled before he left. Liam noticed that Wally did not say anything about a job, but Liam decided not to give up hope, and if Wally and Dakota asked him to leave in the morning, then he'd go. But at least for tonight, he'd sleep in a real bed like a real person rather than the trash that everyone seemed to kick out of their lives. Pulling back the covers, Liam turned off the light before climbing into the comfortable bed and closing his eyes. The shower, the food, and the comfort all worked on him to the point where he almost instantly fell asleep.

LIGHT streaming through the windows woke him, and Liam stretched, cracking his eyes open, and for a few moments he tried to remember where he was and why he wasn't sleeping outside and shivering. Then he remembered, and he didn't want to get out of the bed, but his bladder called to him, as did his stomach. Getting up, Liam walked across the hall to the bathroom, where he took care of business before following the scent of food through the house and into the kitchen. "Good morning," a strange man said, and Liam looked around for Wally or Dakota. "Don't worry. Wally and Dakota are out riding together. They probably won't be back until the end of the day. I'm Phillip, Wally's best friend. Come on in and sit down. I've got some lunch ready for you."

"Lunch?" Liam asked, looking around for a clock.

"Yeah, it's after one," Phillip told him with a grin before putting a plate in front of him. "You must have been tired."

Liam watched as Phillip returned to the sink, cleaning up the dishes. "Do you work here?" he asked between ravenous bites.

"My partner, Haven, owns the ranch with Dakota and Wally," Phillip explained, and Liam nearly dropped his fork. "And before you ask, no, not everyone on the ranch is gay. Just most of us." Phillip laughed softly.

"Is that okay with everyone? I mean, in the town."

Phillip shrugged. "Some people have a problem with us, but we help our neighbors when they need it. I think people have come to see that we're like them. As Wally says, it's hard to hate someone when you know them."

Liam shook his head. In his experience, what Phillip was telling him was hard to believe, but he knew Phillip wasn't lying.

"Finish your lunch. Wally and Dakota said that if you'd stick around, they would like to talk to you when they get home." Phillip finished the dishes and wiped his hands. "I'll be right back." Phillip left the room, and Liam stared, his heart jumping at the thought that they might offer him a job. He tried not to get his hopes up, but it was hard.

The front door opened and then the screen banged shut, making Liam jump. "Where's Phillip?" a strange man asked him in a hurried tone. Before Liam could answer, Phillip returned, pushing a man in a wheelchair.

"What's wrong, Haven?"

"I just got a call from the sheriff. We have cattle all over the road near the west range. Looks like something spooked part of the herd, and they trampled the fence."

Liam forgot about the food. "Are they still on the move?" The man stared at him as Liam's instincts took over.

"Not sure. I need to get out there."

"I can help," Liam volunteered, and he saw the man look at Phillip with a perplexed look.

"Come on, then. Phillip, call Wally and Dakota and have them find us. Dakota knows where we'll be." The man turned to Liam. "Let's go. We'll grab the rest of the men."

Liam followed the man outside to a large shed across from the barn where a number of ATVs were parked, ready for use. The man motioned toward one, and Liam pulled on the helmet before starting it up. Others approached, and soon there was a chorus of throaty engines zooming out of the drive and down the road. Liam followed where the others went. He had no idea who any of these men were, other than Mario, who'd jumped onto one of the machines, but that didn't matter, at least not right now.

Liam's heart pounded a mile a minute as they got farther from the house, and eventually he could see the flattened trail where the cattle had spooked. They followed it, veering to both sides until they came across part of the herd, and they slowed down, letting their engines idle. "Damn it!" the man from the house swore. "It's going to take us all day to get the stupid animals back."

"Not if we can get around them. If we start at the far end, we can probably drive the herd back onto itself and pick up most of them. Then we'll just need to round up the stragglers," Liam offered, and the other men looked at him, some of them nodding.

"Well, then, let's do it," Haven called before issuing instructions, and they took off in different directions, surrounding the herd, and the beasts began to move back the way they'd come. As they approached the downed fence, Liam saw two men on horseback riding toward them. They approached Haven, the three of them talking as they continued driving the cattle back toward the range. Looking toward the others, Liam saw Haven pointing at him as he talked to the men on horseback, who he now recognized as Wally and Dakota. Liam kept his attention on his task, helping to keep the cattle moving in the right direction.

Once they were in the range, some of the men zoomed away after the stragglers, and Liam looked around for some sort of instruction. "Can you fix fences?" he heard Haven yell over to him, and Liam nodded. He could do just about anything on a ranch. Haven motioned for him to follow, and they rode back toward the break before turning off the engines.

A number of the posts had been trampled and bent. "Looks like it's shot and everything will need to be replaced," Liam commented as he surveyed the damage.

"Afraid you're right. Dakota and Wally rode back to the ranch to get supplies. I'm Haven, by the way." He took off his gloves and extended his hand. "Dakota said you needed a job. We have one if you want it, but I have to warn you, the job's kind of different. You'll help out on the ranch, but most of the time, you'll be working with Wally. He's the local vet and a sucker for any animal that needs help."

Liam was confused. "I know all about critters, been around them all my life, but I don't know anything about being a vet."

Haven laughed. "Wally will show you what you need to know."

Liam wasn't quite sure what he was getting himself into, but he needed a job bad, and this place seemed like what he needed. "I'll do my best."

"I know you will," Haven said with a curious smile that Liam couldn't read, and Haven must have read his expression because he continued. "I know what you've been feeling because I was in a similar position."

"How can you possibly know?" Liam asked defiantly, narrowing his eyes. "I've been through things I can't begin to talk about, and you meet me for a few hours and know what I'm feeling?" Liam's gut tightened, and he cringed inwardly. Haven had just offered him a job on a ranch with other gay people, and he was yelling at the man.

"I know, Liam. My father hated Dakota's father and Dakota. Simply put, my father hated them and he would have hated me for being gay. But he died before I told him. I know what it's like to be beaten down to the point where you'd rather lay down and die than go on. I think at some point, most everyone on the ranch did."

Liam felt his emotions bubble to the surface, and he turned away so Haven wouldn't see his vulnerability. He'd learned early on from his father that any weakness would be exploited. Haven touched his shoulder lightly. "I won't ask what happened to you. Not because I don't care. There are plenty of people, including myself, who'll listen when you're ready." Liam felt Haven's fingers tighten slightly before his hand slipped away.

"Thank you," Liam said softly, not trusting his voice not to betray how he was feeling. He could hardly believe he'd gone from basically lying on the side of the road, waiting to die, to finding a job at a place where he just might be accepted for who he was. Liam had spent his life hiding who he was—deeply hiding—and the few times he'd ever taken a chance, he'd gotten grief piled on top of misery for it.

"Let's get this fencing cleaned up so when Wally and Dakota get here with the supplies we can get this repaired as soon as possible." Almost before Haven had finished speaking, a truck rumbled down the road, stopping near where they stood. Haven started to unload the truck, and Liam, grateful to have something to do, began helping as well. Haven handed him a pair of wire cutters, and he started cutting the broken wire from the posts, gathering it into a bundle he could carry. Then he worked the bent posts out of their holes, adding those to the pile of scrap. By the time he was done, the new posts had been set close to where they were going to go, and Dakota and Haven had already begun digging the holes. With the four of them, they had the posts in place and were ready to patch the hole as some of the other hands drove the stragglers back through the break.

"Have you got them all?" Dakota asked a dust-covered Mario once he throttled down the ATV he was riding.

"There are still a few we need to find, and the guys are rounding them up. Since they're closer, they'll move them into the range area nearest them so you can close the hole." Mario turned around and gunned his engine, zipping across the land as the four of them ran and attached the barbed wire to the fence posts.

"Looks like you had an exciting day," Wally said once they were done. "Did Haven speak with you about a job?" he asked, and Liam nodded, smiling even as he wondered just what kind of job he was being offered. "Good. Let's get back to the house, and we can go over your daily chores." Wally's phone rang and he fished it out of his pocket, taking the call before hanging up. "Looks like that will need to wait. Dakota, I need to ride back to the ranch." They threw the tools in the back of the truck, and within minutes, the truck was bounding away.

"Wally's a vet," Haven explained as he looked over their work before climbing onto his ATV. "You get used to the calls."

"Dakota said he was a doctor," Liam commented quietly.

"Dakota's finishing his residency, so he's still gone quite a bit of the time. I believe he's only home for the weekend, and then we won't see him for almost another month." Haven walked toward his ATV, and Liam followed. They rode back to the house together, parking their ATVs in the equipment shed. "Go on inside. You've had a rough few days, and Wally will kill me if I work you to death on your first day." Haven hurried toward the barn, and Liam looked around him, his head still spinning at the turn of his luck.

Inside the house, everything appeared quiet. The man he'd seen earlier in the wheelchair was in the living room, asleep in his chair. "Young man." Liam guessed he wasn't as asleep as he appeared. "Are you Liam?" His voice was slurred, but Liam could understand him.

"Yes, sir," Liam answered.

"I'm Jefferson, Dakota's daddy. He told me about you before he left this morning." A woman in a nurse's uniform came into the room.

"I have your bed changed and ready for you. Do you want to stay here or go back to bed?"

Jefferson's head lolled to the side. "Why would I want to go back to bed? I can sleep when I'm dead."

Liam stifled a laugh as the nurse rolled her eyes. "That's fine, you old coot," she teased affectionately. "Then I'm going to get the rest of my work done. If you get tired, have this young man come get me." She left the room, and Liam sat on the sofa next to Jefferson, wondering what he should be doing. It didn't feel right to be just sitting around.

"It's hell getting old, young man," Jefferson said with a sigh.

"Is there anything I can get for you?"

"A beer," Jefferson answered, and Liam was about to get up when Wally came in the house.

"You know that alcohol messes with your medication," Wally scolded lightly, and Liam could tell Wally had a great deal of affection for Jefferson. "Did you meet Liam? He's going to be working here."

"Yes," Jefferson answered, and Liam saw the older man's eyes begin to close. Not wanting to wake him, Liam followed Wally out of the room and eventually out the back door.

"What is that?" Liam asked, pointing toward what appeared to be fenced cages at the back of the property.

"Those are your new job," Wally answered mischievously. "Would you like to meet them? We have a large-animal rescue," Wally went on to explain. "What I need you to do is help take care of these guys." Wally started walking across the grass, and as they approached the cages, Liam blinked a few times.

"Is that a lion?" Liam could hardly believe his eyes.

Wally laughed softly. "We have three lions and four tigers right now. I try to find permanent homes for them with zoos and animal parks, but some of these guys are so old, no one wants them." Wally stepped close to one of the doors and watched as a large male lion with an impressive mane loped over to him, yawning. "This is Manny. He's getting quite old, but don't let him fool you or think he's a pet, because he's a wild animal, and unpredictable. The first lion I got was Schian, and he loved to have his belly scratched. He was the only one I ever trusted enough to be in the cage with, and even then I was always wary. He died a little over a year ago." Liam saw the loss momentarily in Wally's expression, and he couldn't help wondering what a full-grown lion looked and sounded like when he had his belly scratched.

"What do you want me to do with them?" Liam took a step back from the cage as Manny let out a roar that echoed over the land before settling back down onto the ground. "You must think I'm crazy."

Wally chuckled again. "You need to be wary and careful, but never afraid. Manny is just reminding himself that he's a big boy. He thinks all these cats are part of his pride and that he's the head honcho." Wally moved to the next cage. "There are four enclosures in each group, with a shared exercise area. All you need to do is open the gate in the cage, and they'll amble out when they're ready. I try to give each one a chance in the yard every day." Wally stopped at an enclosure with the most beautiful cat Liam had ever seen.

"Wow," Liam mouthed.

"She's impressive, isn't she? That's Shahrazad. She's a Bengal tiger. She's also the biggest bitch I've ever had. Don't get too close to the enclosure under any circumstances," Wally warned.

Liam had no intention of getting anywhere near her. "Then how do you feed her?" Liam asked tentatively, and Wally opened a chute in the back of the cage. "The food goes in here and the water here." Wally showed him what he needed to do. "Once every few days, we enclose each animal in the common area and clean its cage." Wally stopped talking and looked at Liam appraisingly. "Do you think you can do this? It requires vigilance and patience."

Liam nodded slowly. "I never thought I'd be taking care of lions and tigers."

"There's more," Wally explained, and he began to lead him away. By the time Wally had told him all about the care of big cats and the other exotic animals he had, Liam's head was spinning. "I know this is a lot, so we'll work together for a while. I'm not expecting you to do this alone, but I get called away, and I don't want to worry about their care."

"I can do it," Liam answered with more confidence than he felt. If it meant food and a roof over his head, Liam could do just about anything. Manny roared again, making Liam jump slightly, and then all the other cats began growling, and Liam saw many of them pacing their cages. "What's wrong?"

"I don't know. They sense something. Look at the way their ears are down and their hair stands on edge. Something has them all a bit spooked." Wally began looking around; Liam did as well.

"There's smoke," Liam said, pointing up into the hills surrounding the ranch. "The wind must be carrying the scent this way. It doesn't look like the forest is on fire."

"No, but that's still a lot of smoke, and as dry as it's been, that fire could spread and take out the entire ranch and half the valley." Wally was already hurrying back toward the house.

"What are you going to do?' Liam asked as he followed behind, and Wally stopped, like he hadn't thought that far ahead. "Like I said, I don't think the forest is on fire—the smoke isn't moving or spreading. If you tell me the way, I could try to go up there and see what's up," Liam offered. He didn't want to sit around doing nothing when he could be of help.

"There's not much up there. I think Dakota told me once that there was a track up there at the end of the road on the west edge of the ranch, but I've never been up there." Wally turned and looked at the smoke again, worry plain on his face.

"Is it okay if I take one of the ATVs? I can ride out there and see what's going on. It shouldn't take very long," Liam offered, and Wally nodded absently. There wasn't any reason to assume it was anything other than someone camping up there, although it seemed to Liam that there was too much smoke for just a campfire.

"Go on, but be careful," Wally cautioned, still looking worried.

Liam hurried to the equipment shed and hopped on the ATV he'd used before, grateful that he was doing something that didn't involve animals that could rip him apart. He started the engine and pulled out of the shed, traveling along the road in front of the ranch before turning down a dirt road at the end of the range that went back toward the hills. The warm, dry air ruffled his hair as he opened the throttle until the road appeared to end at a path just wide enough to allow the ATV to pass. Liam slowed and began to climb steadily up the hillside. Through breaks in the overgrowth, Liam could occasionally see the plume of smoke getting closer and closer.

Liam drove carefully, mindful of washouts and limbs across the path. A few times, he had to move limbs before he could pass, and as the trail got thinner, Liam began to wonder how he'd turn around if he couldn't go any further. Then the trail dumped him onto what looked like a two-track that appeared to have been used recently, and Liam turned. He hadn't gone far before he began to smell the odor of something unpleasant burning. Liam wrinkled his nose as he continued up the path, the scent becoming more pervasive and strong enough that his eyes began to water and his nose to run. *What in the hell could be burning?*

Finally, Liam rode to the edge of a clearing where he saw a large fire burning in a pit, the smell making him gag, and he tried his best not to throw up. Of course, he forgot all about that when he saw a man approach him, a rifle leveled at his chest. Liam didn't know what to say and sat totally still as he watched the man walk toward him. "What are you doing here?"

"I… we saw the fire, and it was dry, so I was just checking it out," Liam answered nervously and watched as the gun wavered for a second before slowly lowering.

"You've done that, so now I suggest you leave."

Relieved that the man was no longer pointing a gun at him, Liam looked at him and felt his mouth drop open. He removed his helmet to get a better look. Beneath the rough clothing and hard eyes was the most beautiful man Liam had ever laid eyes on.

Chapter Two

TROY might have lowered his gun, but he still kept a close eye on the stunning young man who had suddenly shown up outside his small cabin. Troy forced himself to look away. It was not keeping his thoughts on what was important in life that had gotten him into the mess he was in now. "You really should go," Troy reiterated and waited for the boy to start up his engine and tool away.

"What are you burning? It smells like death."

Troy turned around and saw the younger man wrinkle his nose, and he caught himself before he could smile. Damn, the man was cute. But that didn't really matter.

"Water got into the cabin through an open window, and most of the stuff inside got wet and molded, so I need to burn it all," Troy explained. "And now that your curiosity has been satisfied, you can go." Troy walked back inside the cabin and hauled out a small chair before tossing it on the burning pile.

"You really should have something handy in case the fire gets out of control. Everything around here is so dry, you could start the entire area on fire."

Troy whirled around, glaring at the kid without giving him an answer before returning to his work. He figured the kid would leave on his own if Troy ignored him. Walking to the cabin, he looked around the small space. At least that was the last of the crap from inside, and now that he'd made the repairs to the building, he could let the cabin dry out before bringing in his meager possessions. Leaving the door open, Troy went back outside and watched the fire as it consumed the last of the furniture and crap from the cabin. Troy had to admit that it had smelled like death, and at least that particular portion of this chore seemed to be winding down. Looking across the clearing, he saw the young man still watching him. "You can go now," Troy called out, and he watched as the kid climbed back on his ATV, started the engine, and then disappeared down the hill, the sound of the motor fading in the distance. The only sound remaining was the dying roar of the bonfire and the crackling as it collapsed onto itself.

Troy walked to his old truck and pulled out a small tent, setting it up near the cabin. Lucky for him, Troy had doubted that his uncle's hunting cabin would be habitable, so he'd come prepared. He unrolled a foam pad and then a sleeping bag before going back to the truck for a few more things. His bed made up, Troy cooked himself some dinner and then sat in the quiet clearing as his bonfire died away and night descended around him. Yawning widely, Troy pushed some of the dirt he'd dug out of his makeshift firepit into the hole to douse any lingering flames before climbing into his tent to sleep. Instead, he lay in his sleeping bag and listened to the sounds of the night, but eventually he fell asleep.

THE sun illuminating the canvas woke him, and Troy stretched before climbing out of the tent. The first thing he did, after answering the call of nature, that is, was check the inside of the cabin. At least the place smelled better, but one thing Troy had not brought with him was cleaning supplies, and he needed to make sure everything was washed before he actually moved into the cabin.

Walking over to the large pit in the clearing, Troy made sure the fire was out, reminding himself to fill it in later in the day. Then he walked to his truck, such as it was, and climbed into the driver's seat before starting the engine and carefully turning around and slowly driving the track down the mountain.

It took a while to get to town, mainly because Troy hadn't been to the area in years and many of the landmarks he'd remembered as a kid were gone and he didn't want to make the wrong turn like he had once already. He'd been lucky two days ago to have actually found the place at all. That first night, after nearly getting lost, it had been evening when he'd arrived. The cabin a been such a mess that he'd spent that night at a hotel and then spent the entire day yesterday making repairs and cleaning out the damaged contents. With all the activity, Troy hadn't had much chance to think, but now that he was alone in the truck, the road flowing beneath the wheels, his mind wandered, which was something he'd been trying desperately to stop from happening for months. He'd made a complete mess of his life and the lives of those he'd loved most: his wife and his daughter. Tears came to his eyes as he thought about them and the looks on their shattered faces. Troy saw those looks every night after he went to bed and every time he allowed his mind to wander. His attention returned to the present as the outskirts of town appeared in his windshield. Feeling around in the door pocket, Troy found a napkin and wiped his eyes with it as he approached the town.

Parking outside the same small hardware store he'd stopped at yesterday to buy the repair supplies for the cabin, Troy turned off the engine before stepping onto the sidewalk and thunking the truck door closed. The air felt so fresh and clean, and it almost made Troy feel that way as well—almost. Looking up, Troy saw himself reflected in the store window and knew that nothing would ever really make him clean. That just wasn't possible. Troy turned away from his reflection because he couldn't stand to look at it. He hadn't been able to do that since the day, months ago, when his brother had forced him to face who he really was. Pulling open the door, Troy walked inside, a bell jingling as the door closed automatically behind him.

Troy found himself inches from a man carrying a bag in his hands and tried to step out of the way, but he was too late, and they bumped into one another. The man lifted his eyes, and Troy nearly gasped when he saw the same rich blue he'd seen the day before. Troy stopped for a second, unable to move or think, and the man seemed to react the same way. "S…

sorry," he stammered and tried to step around him, and Troy stepped the same way. Their feet caught each other, and Troy stumbled, catching himself on the counter before he fell. "Sorry," the man said again.

"It was my fault," Troy responded automatically before stepping to the side to let him pass. For a few seconds, their eyes met, but Troy looked away, letting his eyes travel to the floor. This was wrong, and being attracted to another man had only ever caused him pain. For the millionth time, he wondered why he had to be like this. Why couldn't he be like everyone else? That was all he'd ever wanted, to be normal. The bell ringing as the door opened again pulled Troy out of his thoughts, and he saw the young man standing in the open doorway with another man behind him. Troy backed up to let them enter and then cleared his mind, trying to remember the things he needed.

"Wally, that's the man I told you about," Troy heard as they walked away, and he saw the other man turn and glare at him. For a second, Troy thought he was going to approach him, so he hurried down one of the aisles.

"He's the one who threatened you with a gun?" The voice was not happy, and Troy expected to be confronted. He didn't really have an excuse for his behavior, not that the gun had even been loaded. Troy heard more soft conversation over the counter that he couldn't make out, and he decided to ignore it, get the things he needed, and get back to the cabin. Troy found a handbasket at the end of the aisle and began filling it with heavy-duty cleaners as well as sponges, cloths, paper towels, and a scrub brush and bucket. He also grabbed a mop and headed toward the counter. As he waited to pay, the other two men got in line behind him, and Troy could almost feel stares on his back. Not that he didn't deserve it—he'd just heard someone coming onto his property and overreacted.

When his turn came, Troy paid for his purchases and hurried out of the store to his truck, placing his bags behind the seat before driving away as quickly as he could. On his way out of town, Troy saw a grocery store and pulled into the parking lot. At least the cabin had electricity, as well as an old refrigerator that seemed to work, and Troy hoped he could get it clean.

Walking across the parking lot, Troy grabbed a cart and began shopping. Knowing he could come back into town, Troy got enough food for just a few days before approaching the meat department, where he saw the people from the hardware store waiting at the counter. Troy was just about to hurry away when the shorter man saw him and strode over in his direction. "You know, it wasn't very nice to point a gun at Liam. He was only trying to make sure the fire wasn't out of control." The short man's eyes blazed at Troy. "What were you thinking?"

"Sorry," Troy muttered. "It wasn't loaded," he added as an explanation, but he knew it sounded lame. "I shouldn't have done that." Now that he'd apologized, Troy wanted to get away as quickly as he could, but it appeared that the man in front of him had other ideas.

"Wally, it's fine," the man with the deep blue eyes said uncomfortably.

"No, it's not, Liam. This isn't the Old West, and people should not be threatening people for no reason. Anyway, checking to see that a fire doesn't threaten the entire valley is a perfectly valid reason and does not give him the right to point a gun at you regardless of whether it's loaded or not."

"Wally. He didn't mean anything by it, and he didn't hurt me. So please let it be," Liam said, and Troy saw Wally look at the other man protectively. At first, Troy thought Wally wasn't going to let it go, but then he turned and walked back to the meat counter, glaring over his shoulder at Troy before the butcher began handing them large packages in white paper.

"That should hold your kitties over for a few days, doc, but if it doesn't, give us a call and we'll have some more for you," the butcher said with a smile, and Troy watched as Liam loaded the packages into the cart. Troy couldn't help wondering just how many cats this was supposed to feed, especially since the butcher was passing over what looked like enough meat for a small army.

"Thanks, Carl. We'll do that. Otherwise, we'll see you early next week. Liam is helping me now, so he'll most likely be the one coming in," Wally explained, and the two of them moved away. Troy approached the counter, placing his order and waiting while the butcher wrapped it in paper. Troy took it and headed for the checkout. It was a small store, and there was only one lane open. Troy got in line and once again ended up in line with Wally and Liam. Troy saw Liam turn around, and Troy was struck again by how handsome Liam was, and how his gaze seemed to bore straight into him. Troy shifted nervously, because the thought that someone might be able to see through him to the shame and self-loathing he felt was almost too much for him to take.

"I'm sorry about yesterday," Troy said softly, and he saw Liam nod slightly before turning back to his cart, loading the contents on the belt. Troy noticed that Liam kept looking at him, and he wondered what exactly it meant. At first, he sort of figured Liam was nervous about him, but from the way he seemed to be looking at him, that couldn't be it. Liam's eyes shone, and for a second, Troy smiled back at him, feeling a slight hitch in his stomach, but he forced that touch of excitement away. He could not allow any feelings like this; that was the way he'd lost everything in the first place. Turning away, Troy focused his attention on his basket of groceries, but he still found himself looking at Liam through his eyelashes. He'd already noticed the younger man's blue eyes, but his long, auburn hair and high cheekbones made him look like some sort of model, at least to Troy, and he had a hard time looking away from him. Not that it really mattered.

Liam and Wally paid for their groceries and left the store, with Liam looking back at him for just a moment. Troy loaded the contents of his cart on the belt and waited while the cashier rang them up before bagging and carrying them out to the truck.

Troy drove back to the cabin, eating cold cereal for breakfast before getting to work. There was still so much to do. The cabin was only a large, open room with a kitchen and living room, plus a bedroom and bath. Troy decided he needed to start with the bathroom and girded himself to take on the mess. An hour later, the fixtures were clean and the place no longer smelled of rot. Then he moved to the bedroom, scrubbing down everything before tackling the kitchen and living areas. "Hello in there," someone called from outside, and he nearly grabbed the gun from by the door, but that had worked so well last time that he left it where it was. Walking to the door, Troy opened it and saw a big man standing near the remains of his firepit, staring back at him.

"What do you want?" Troy asked as he stared back.

"You nearly scared one of my hands to death yesterday, and I wanted to know why," the man said firmly. "Furthermore, I'd like to know what you're doing here."

"I'm here because I own this place, and I already apologized to your hand when I was in town today," Troy responded firmly before turning to go back inside. He'd moved up here to be alone, but he'd been here two days, and he'd already had more visitors than in the months before he left the East Coast.

"This is Max Hunter's place," the man said.

Troy huffed but figured that maybe once he'd answered the man's questions he'd go away and leave him alone. "He was my uncle, and he died," Troy said matter-of-factly before adding, "and who are you?"

"I'm Dakota Holden. My ranch is at the base of the hill."

Something in Troy's distant memory jogged free. "Dakota." He actually felt a smile cross his face. "You probably don't remember me. I'm Troy. We met when I came to the cabin with Uncle Max one summer. I must have been eight, I guess. You were probably about six. I don't expect you to remember me." Hell, Troy barely remembered Dakota, except that it was the only time in his life when he'd ever ridden a horse, and things like that tended to stick in your mind.

Dakota's expression softened considerably, even though he shook his head. "I wish I could say I did, but I really don't remember you at all." Dakota stepped closer. "What are you doing here?"

"This is where I live, at least for now." Troy had no intention of explaining anything more than that. Troy stepped out of the doorway and walked to where Dakota stood. "I really didn't mean to scare your hand. He actually seemed nice."

"You're planning to live in your uncle's hunting cabin? You know you really can't do that over the winter. You won't be able to get in and out of here for months at a time. Once the snow starts, it often falls by the foot, and the road isn't plowed, let alone the track up here."

Troy sighed softly. He should have known that, but after living all those years on the East Coast, he'd never considered how harsh the winters could be. Troy looked around at the quiet clearing and the cabin, figuring he had months to figure out what he wanted to do. "Right now I just want some peace and quiet."

Dakota nodded slowly. "Okay, that's your right. If you want some company or need anything, we're at the base of the hill." Dakota turned and began walking down the track through the woods. Troy watched him go and wondered if he'd actually walked the entire way up here, but after a few minutes he heard the low rumble of an engine starting and then quieting as it got farther away. Slowly turning back toward the house, he walked inside and went to work.

Once the cleaning was done, Troy opened the tailgate of the covered bed of the truck and began pulling out his few belongings. It wasn't much, but at least he had a bed and some kitchen essentials. By the time evening settled around him, he was all set in his small cabin. Pulling his single chair outside, Troy sat beside the back door and watched as night descended around him. All day he'd been busy, and now the quiet surrounded him, with only the sounds of the woods. He'd wanted peace and quiet, and he'd wanted to be alone, but Troy quickly discovered that he could travel to a place where his nearest neighbor was miles away and yet he could not travel away from his thoughts and his guilt. Troy *was* guilty; he knew that. He'd broken Jeanie's heart, and he'd lied to everyone in his life. Nothing could make up for that and nothing could change that. Troy had figured out during the months after the fallout from his revelation that he wasn't fit to be around anyone, so when Uncle Max had died and left Kevin and him the cabin, he'd decided to come West and lose himself in the open space. He just wished he could quiet his mind and find some of the peace he craved so badly. But very little had gone the way he'd planned.

Troy sat for hours, alone with thoughts he didn't want to be thinking, but his mind would not let them go. Finally, Troy gave up and went inside, stripping down before cleaning up as best he could and climbing into bed. Maybe tomorrow would be better.

It wasn't. Troy got up with the sun, ate, and then got to work. There was wood to be chopped and other chores to do. Once he had a good pile of logs stacked away from the cabin, Troy went to work filling in the rest of the pit he'd used for the fire before spreading the remaining dirt around the clearing and filling any holes. The activity was fine, but whenever he stopped, his thoughts took over again. "Two fucking days," Troy said out loud. He'd been here two days and he was already tired of his own company and his own thoughts—some loner he turned out to be. He should have known this was not going to work. He'd always been a rather social person, and if being alone all the time was already getting to him, what was he going to do for the next four months? Sit around his cabin, grow a beard, and watch the trees grow? It occurred to him that this was not the brightest idea he'd ever had. But on the other hand, he could barely look at himself in the mirror—how was he supposed to face other people, especially once they found out what he'd done? No, he was just going to need to get used to being alone, and he was going to need to figure out how to keep himself occupied.

Troy managed to keep busy for almost a week. In that time, he actually managed to build a few pieces of rustic furniture, and he even made a trip down the hill to fish in one of the small streams that ran into the river. He'd caught a few fish and cooked them for himself, but after nearly a week, he was starting to tire of his own company big-time. Troy knew he could go to town and maybe get something other than his own cooking to eat, but Dakota had also said they were there if he wanted company.

Somehow, Troy doubted Dakota had really meant what he said, but he was getting desperate. Maybe he could pay them a visit, be neighborly, and since he still had a few of the fish cleaned and in the refrigerator, maybe he could take a peace offering while he was at it. Troy admitted to himself that he still felt bad about the way he'd treated Liam that first day. Troy just wasn't certain how he'd be welcomed or how he felt about just popping in on his neighbors, especially ones that he'd made such a *wonderful* impression on. However, he wasn't sure what else to do, and at least he knew Dakota from when they were kids, kind of.

Troy went inside the cabin, making a stop in the bathroom to scrape the stubble from his face. Then he cleaned up before taking the fish from the refrigerator and heading out toward the truck. He somehow figured he was being a little crazy in doing this, but he knew no one else. Before getting in the truck, Troy looked around the clearing for what had to be the millionth time since he'd arrived. He already knew each tree and shrub. He was lucky he hadn't actually named them yet. No, for his sanity he had to spend some time around other people. Afterward, he could always return to the quiet of the cabin. Opening the truck door, Troy got inside and started the engine before descending the hill, bouncing over the ruts in the two-track before finally making it to the road. It still took him a while before he made it to the main road, and then he wondered which way to turn. Dakota really hadn't told him exactly where the ranch was, something Troy wished he'd thought of before he'd acted. But lately, that seemed to be the pattern of his life. In the past six months, he'd been acting before he thought on a regular basis, and that was something else that had to change. Troy thought of turning around and going home. Instead, he turned left and hoped for the best.

A while later, Troy pulled up in front of what looked like a ranch house and stopped the truck. He hoped he was in the right place. Getting out, he picked up the wrapped fish and stepped slowly toward the front door. It opened to reveal the man he'd seen in the grocery store, Wally, glaring at him.

"I'm sorry, I must—" Troy was about to say he thought he had the wrong place, but he knew he didn't. This man had scolded him, and so had Dakota. He had the right ranch, and from the look on Wally's face, he wasn't at all welcome. "Is this the Holden ranch?"

"Yes," Wally answered as he stepped closer. "I should pull a gun on you so you can feel what it's like." Wally continued moving closer to him. "Instead, I'll tell you to get the hell off my land and leave us alone." Troy turned and opened his truck door. He should have expected a reaction like this; hell, he probably deserved it. "What are you doing here?" Troy didn't really have an answer. He simply handed Wally the package of fish, got back into his truck, and hurried out of the drive and back up to the cabin where he belonged. At least now he remembered exactly why he'd wanted to get away from everyone. Parking outside the cabin, Troy went inside and closed the door behind him. This was all his fault, he knew that, just like the complete and utter mess that he'd made of his life was all his fault.

A quiet knock on the door pulled Troy out of his pity party, and he opened the door, wondering who wanted to chastise him now. What he saw was a pair of bright eyes and a beautiful, nervous-looking face smiling back at him. "I can only say I'm sorry so many times."

"Huh?" Liam said, the smile on his face fading slightly. "Oh. No, we owe you an apology this time," Liam said softly. "I know you didn't know who I was that day, and Wally's being a little protective. Dakota says he gets that way sometimes. It's part of what makes him a good vet and a good friend. I'm Liam, by the way."

"I know. I heard Wally say your name in the store," Troy said, looking into those deep blue eyes and finding himself getting lost for just a few seconds. "Does Wally know you're here?"

"Yes," Wally answered as he stepped into the doorway. "I think we both could learn a few lessons about being more neighborly." To Troy's surprise, Wally looked a bit contrite. "I wanted to thank you for the fish.

That was very nice of you." Troy thought that the words looked almost painful for Wally.

"I know I overreacted the other day, and I apologize for that. I shouldn't have pulled a gun on him. I didn't know why he was here, but I shouldn't have assumed he was a threat."

Liam and Wally sort of stared at him as the conversation trailed off. "Um, why did you come to the ranch?" Wally asked. "Did you need something?"

Troy shrugged. He thought of saying that he wanted a little company, but it sounded needy and a little dumb. Thankfully, Wally didn't wait for an answer.

"Look, to be neighborly, why don't you join us at the ranch for dinner? We can talk things over and hopefully put this behind us. We are neighbors, after all."

"Thanks," Troy answered before stepping away from the door. "Would you like to come in? The place isn't much." Troy tried to think if he had anything to serve to drink, but all he could come up with was water.

"No, thank you," Wally answered. "We need to get back to work, but we'll see you about six for dinner." Wally nodded, and Troy watched as the two of them crossed to the truck parked next to his, particularly scrutinizing every move Liam made. Once the other men were in the truck, Troy closed the door and the guilt began. Troy knew he was attracted to Liam, and he sort of thought that Liam was gay. He wasn't sure why he felt that way, but he did. Troy also knew that he could never allow anything to come of the feelings that seemed to bloom in him whenever he saw the other man. That was where his life had fallen apart in the first place. It was those feelings, and his inability to control them, that had caused all the pain in his life.

Troy pushed the guilt back and went to work. He had to try to be around others, and he knew he couldn't let his past mistakes rule the rest of his life. He had to move past his own insecurities if he was going to be able to have any type of life, not that he felt he deserved one.

Troy kept himself as busy as he could for the rest of the afternoon. He decided to go fishing again and managed to catch two more mountain trout, which he cleaned and put in the refrigerator for later in the week. Since he wasn't working, he needed to make the money he had last as long as he could. Troy cleaned up and dug around in his bag to find some clothes that appeared reasonably nice before dressing and then leaving the cabin for the ride to the ranch. This time when he arrived, Troy was greeted by a pack of dogs, their tails wagging their backsides as they barked and climbed over one another for attention. "Okay, guys, that's enough," Liam said as he walked across the yard to meet Troy. The dogs immediately changed tactics, swarming around Liam's feet, and two seconds later, he'd half fallen to the ground as the dogs licked, wagged, and squirmed around him in complete doggie delight. Troy could not take his eyes off Liam as the dogs showed their own love.

"Come on, guys," Wally said from the steps before whistling, and the pack raced toward the house, stopping at the base of the steps and looking up at Wally expectantly. Troy walked to where Liam sat on the ground and extended his hand to help him up. As soon as he touched the other man, a zing went through him, and Troy nearly let go in surprise, afraid of what the feeling could mean. Troy helped Liam to his feet and then let go of his hand a little faster than he wanted, seeing disappointment pass across Liam's face, but Troy had promised himself that he was going to keep his feelings under control, and he couldn't do that if he touched Liam. That simple touch made his heart race, and he could feel himself sweating from just holding the man's hand. Troy followed Liam toward the house and up the steps, doing his best to keep his gaze off the tight jeans that hugged Liam's butt perfectly.

"Would you like something to drink?" Wally asked once they were seated in the living room. Wally left and returned with a beer for everyone. He then left again, and returned pushing a wheelchair. "Jefferson, this is Troy. He's staying in the old cabin on the mountain."

"Max's place?" Jefferson asked, and Troy had to listen carefully in order to understand him.

"Yes. Uncle Max died a few months ago and left the cabin to my brother and me. I'm staying there for now," Troy explained. He remembered Mr. Holden from when he was a child, and how he'd lifted him up so Troy could sit on the huge horse, and then he'd led him all around the yard. But that had been a long time ago, and a lot had changed.

"If you don't mind my asking, why are you living in the cabin?" Liam asked quietly, but Troy could feel his eyes on him.

"I wanted some peace and some time to think, but it hasn't worked out the way I planned," Troy admitted.

"How so?" Wally asked as he sat on the sofa next to Liam.

Troy stared at the top of the beer bottle. "All I do is think about things I can't do anything about. I'm fine when I'm busy, but when I'm not, I keep mulling over the things I was hoping to put behind me."

"You can't run from your problems," Jefferson said, and that Troy understood clearly. He had to admit that the man was right. That was exactly what he'd been trying to do, and it wasn't working.

"What are you running from?" Liam asked, and Troy was saved from answering by the door opening and two men walking in.

"Troy, this is Haven and his partner Phillip. Haven manages the cattle portion of the business, and Phillip does the accounting and helps manage the business end."

Troy found himself staring at the two men and then back at Wally and Liam. Haven and Phillip were a couple, and openly so, like Peter and Kevin. The concept didn't surprise him; he'd seen Kevin and Peter together for years. It was the fact that he was seeing an openly gay couple *here* that threw him.

"Is there a problem?" Wally asked, and Troy pulled his gaze away and back to his beer bottle.

"No," Troy answered softly.

"Do you have a problem with the fact that we're all gay?" Wally's question sounded like a challenge.

"No. My brother is gay. I guess I'm surprised to see an open couple here." The significance of Wally's words took a second to work into his mind. "You're all gay?"

"Yes. Dakota's my partner, and our ranch foreman, Mario, lives with his partner, David," Wally explained as he looked at Troy expectantly. Troy's gaze traveled to each person in the room before settling on Liam, who looked at him like he already knew what was in Troy's heart. He'd felt that way before, but it was even stronger now.

"I'm gay too," Troy said softly, his voice barely above a mumble. No one asked him to repeat what he'd said or say it louder. He might have barely vocalized his secret, but Troy felt as though he'd shouted it. All the others in the room simply nodded. This was a bit eye-opening for Troy. He'd seen what his brother Kevin had gone through, and that was part of the reason he'd determined he wasn't going to put himself through that. Kevin had been picked on constantly in high school. He'd had very few friends and stayed pretty much to himself. There had been no way Troy was going to allow that kind of ostracism for himself. But there was no ostracism here—only what felt like acceptance.

"It's okay," Liam said, barely above a whisper. "This place is like heaven for people like us." Troy turned and caught Liam's eyes and noticed a deep hurt in him that looked and felt so familiar. Troy swallowed as he realized that someone had hurt the younger man very badly.

"Were you always honest and open about who you were?" Troy asked with a touch of disbelief. He couldn't imagine not hiding who he was. He'd been doing it so long, it had become an ingrained habit. Even after telling his wife and facing her wrath, he still hid who he was and tried to hide it from himself.

"Sort of, I guess," Liam answered nervously, and Troy guessed that Liam was in no bigger hurry to discuss his past than Troy was. "But here,

I don't have to worry about that. I've seen Wally and Dakota hug and kiss each other. David and Mario have done the same, as have Phillip and Haven. Here there's no shame or judgment for being who you are, unlike the rest of the world." Liam looked over at Wally, and Troy saw just a bit of hero-worship on his face. For a second, Troy felt his throat dry and his breath shorten. At first, he didn't understand what was happening or what he was feeling, until he realized he was jealous. Just once in his life, Troy had hoped someone would look at him like that. He'd always expected it would be Sofia, but that wasn't likely now. "Wally, is there anything I can help with?" Liam asked before standing up.

"No. Everything is under control. Why don't you take Troy out and show him the animals?"

Troy looked from Wally to Liam, wondering if that was such a good idea. His first instinct was to beg off. The thought of being alone with Liam was almost too much temptation, but he didn't want to have to explain his reluctance, and he also figured it would be impolite to refuse. Everyone was being friendly, and Troy didn't want to jeopardize that—not when it seemed he'd been able to make up for some of his initial bad impression. "Sounds like fun," Troy answered, trying to cover up a rush of excitement as he stood up.

Liam led him out the door, and Troy expected they would go toward the barn, but instead Liam led him around the side of the house and across the back lawn. "Wally runs an animal rescue, and I help him care for the cats." Liam sounded proud, and Troy wondered what could be so rewarding about caring for a bunch of cats, that is, until he saw the enclosures and the huge predators prowling inside. "Don't get too close. Some of them are just big kitties, but most of them are very much still wild animals."

"Where do they come from?" Troy asked as he stared at a huge male lion walking slowly around his enclosure. He was magnificent, and Troy was fascinated at being able to see him this closely. Then his eyes were drawn to the tigers and other large cats in the cages that formed the group of enclosures. "My God."

"That's just what I thought when Wally told me my job was to help care for them. The tiger is Shahrazad, and she's a mean one, so I stay away from her. The lion is Manny, and he rules the roost. They're prowling because you smell different. Wally says they're very smart and sometimes know when things are about to happen. Wally gets them from circuses and people who think they'll make good pets. He told me he's had luck placing some of them in zoos. He's hoping one will take Shahrazad. She's a Bengal and very valuable." The hero-worshiping look was in full force on Liam's face. Obviously Wally had made quite an impression on Liam.

"How long have you been here?" Troy asked as he watched Manny settle onto the grass.

"A little over a week. The day I investigated the fire was my first full day here," Liam answered without looking at him, and Troy felt worse about the way he'd behaved that first day. "I know you didn't know."

"Thanks, but pointing a rifle at you was a great way to say welcome to the neighborhood." Troy made light of the incident to cover how bad he felt about the whole thing.

"Just forget it," Liam said. "It was an accident." Liam watched the animals settle down onto the grass. "Have you ever had a boyfriend?"

Troy wasn't sure how to answer that question, and when he saw Liam turn to look at him, Troy knew he needed to be honest. He'd lied about himself so much the words almost came out on their own. "No. Not really. There was never anyone that I could call a boyfriend. Have you?"

Liam shook his head. "No. I met someone once. My dad caught us kissing, and he made sure I would never do that again. I always wondered what it would be like to have a boyfriend—someone who liked me for me." The sadness in Liam's voice tugged at Troy's heart. He'd made so many people sad that all he wanted to do was make up for it by making Liam's sadness fade. Troy's hand had bridged half the distance between them before he caught himself and let it fall back to his side.

Liam turned around, and Troy saw the longing and pain on Liam's face, and it both surprised and hurt him. He hadn't expected to see the other man's emotions so plain on his face, and then Troy wondered if that was how his ex-wife had looked when she went to live with her sister after his big revelation. Troy closed his eyes for a second, and when he opened them again, the pain was gone, but the longing remained. "You will. Everyone deserves someone who sees you and loves you for you." Troy wasn't sure he believed those words because he wasn't sure he deserved that for himself, but it was what Liam needed to hear. "We should head back inside. I'm not sure what time Wally had planned dinner."

"I suppose," Liam answered softly. "Did you ever feel like you were the only person in the world like this?"

"Yes and no," Troy answered. "I knew I wasn't alone because my brother, Kevin, is gay, and he came out quite young. I wasn't about to go through what he did, so I tried to will myself to be normal, I guess." Troy scoffed lightly. "I wish I could explain it to you, then maybe I could explain it to myself."

"I know how you feel. It's hard to put things in words when you've been hiding them all your life. For years I thought there was no one else in the world like me, that I was some freak of nature. And then the preacher one Sunday talked fire and brimstone about Sodom and Gomorrah, and I realized that maybe I wasn't alone, but that I was evil." Liam stared at Manny, but Troy figured Liam was looking right through him. "But I'm not evil; I'm a good person. Wally and everyone else here helped me see that."

"No, you aren't evil. As long as you're true to yourself and don't hurt other people," Troy clarified, knowing he'd failed on both counts. Suddenly, Troy very much wanted this conversation to end, but it seemed to be what Liam needed. "Kevin says we're born gay, and I believe him. No one would choose to be different or hated. We would all choose to be the same as everyone else. A few years after he came out, Kevin told me that being gay for him was just as much a part of who he was as the color of his eyes or the size of his feet. When he told me that, I almost told him I was gay too. That was the closest I came to telling another person until about six months ago." Troy sighed as he followed Liam's gaze. "Now, looking back on it, I wish I had told him. Maybe my life would have been different." That was true, maybe it would have, if he'd had the courage to admit and stand up for who he was.

"Your brother sounds smart," Liam commented.

"He is. One of the smartest people I know." Troy probably would never have admitted that a few months ago. For as long as he could remember, if Kevin said something, Troy did the opposite. He could not count the number of times that had gotten him into trouble. Troy had discounted his brother for over a decade because he was gay, regardless of the fact that he was obviously the smarter member of the family, and, Troy had to admit, the happier one as well. "I just wish I'd have allowed myself to admit that earlier." If he had, he and Kevin would have had a better relationship, and he might have actually listened and understood what his brother stood for. "And he's courageous. He was willing to live his life no matter what other people thought. That took strength I wish I'd had."

Liam began walking toward the house, and Troy followed. "You're strong," Liam said as they walked, "you just need to figure out how to use it, the same as me." Troy's life experiences certainly made him doubt that statement, but he didn't argue with Liam.

Walking into the house, they seemed to have entered a spirited argument in progress. "You don't know that, Haven," Wally said earnestly. At least the argument seemed to be around a point of opinion, unlike the arguments Troy was used to, which usually degenerated into high drama and God knew what else.

"Yes, I do. When someone gives $80,000 to the community center in a town like ours, they definitely want something. I asked around town today, and no one knows who exactly gave the money except the community center board, but the rumor is that it was a large company of some sort," Haven explained with equal passion. "And why would any company do that? They want something, pure and simple. Ten to one we hear who the donor was just as soon as they decide there's something they want badly enough to spend a bunch of money to get it."

"You're too suspicious, Haven," Wally countered. "You don't even know if the rumor is correct. It could have been someone in town."

Haven scoffed, and Troy settled on the sofa next to Liam, listening in on the discussion. "No, I'm not. This town has been trying to build a community center for years," Haven said. "We've had fundraisers every summer that got us closer, and now suddenly someone comes up with the exact amount needed to complete the project? I don't buy it. Besides, no one in town has that kind of money, except maybe us, and that kind of donation would really strap our operation. The other cattlemen don't have it, and neither do the townsfolk."

"We'll have to wait and see," Wally said calmly before standing up. "I'm going to get dinner. It'll be ready in about fifteen minutes." Wally left the room, and Haven looked expectantly toward Troy.

"So, Troy, what do you think?"

"About what, the community center donation? I don't know anything about it. I've only been here a little over a week, and before that I was here when I was eight. So…." Troy let his thought trail off. "What could anyone want around here besides buying up the land? But if that were the case, why wouldn't they just begin making offers to the landowners?"

Haven smiled, and his face got this excited-puppy look Troy thought Phillip must find endearing as well. "That's just it. There's only one thing I can think of, and that's water rights for something. There's plenty of land around here that's cheap because there's no water. So if someone were to buy up that land and then convince a landowner to lease them or sell them water rights, they could suddenly increase the value and productivity of the land. No rancher would ever do that, though, because that's a good part of the value of our land as well as our livelihood."

Troy found Haven's line of reasoning fascinating, and as he peered at Liam, he could see he was interested as well. "Then why worry about it?"

"Because the town owns water rights on the river that runs through it. It's upstream from us, so if they were to let someone use the water, there would be less left for us, and that means that in July and August, when the river is already at its lowest point, it could be dangerously low for us and anyone downstream."

"So you think whoever made the donation is buttering up the town?" It sounded a bit far-fetched.

"Why would they do that?" Liam asked, and Haven shrugged. "Don't they rely on their ranchers for their livelihood?"

Haven nodded and seemed a little frustrated. Wally's voice drifted in from the kitchen. "We'll have to wait and see. But that doesn't mean we can't listen, and it wouldn't hurt to be a little nosy." Wally walked back into the room. "Besides, even I know how to find out something. Telephone, telegraph, tele-Edie."

"Tele-Edie?" Troy asked.

"Well, more like Ask-an-Edie. She works at the bank and knows everything that goes on in town. If anyone has heard anything about what's up, it's her. So, Haven, I suggest you put on a pair of those tight jeans and pay her a visit if you're so curious," Wally said teasingly as he went back in the kitchen.

"Hey!" Phillip griped and moved closer. "No one else is supposed to be ogling him in those jeans but me." Haven pulled the other man closer and said something into his ear that made Phillip color slightly. Troy watched them together and felt a pang of jealousy. He and Jeanie had never been like that. Even after they were first married, there was a certain reserve that they'd both had. Troy now understood fully where it had come from, but he wondered what it would be like to be that close to someone and to have someone that close to him. Troy looked over at Liam and saw the same longing plain on his face, and when those large blue eyes met his, Troy's breath stopped. Never in his life had he seen such intense attraction in someone else's eyes, and to have it centered on him was both exciting and completely frightening at the same time. He could almost feel Liam moving closer, and Troy knew he probably would not have the willpower to stop him if he did.

The crash of a pan hitting the floor followed by a string of curses that would make a sailor blush broke the mood, and Liam got up and hurried toward the kitchen. "Can we help?" Phillip asked, and Wally's answer was more swearing followed by a "No."

Troy sat where he was and listened to the swearing as it trailed off into some pan-banging. "Dinner will be a few minutes longer," Wally said without coming into the room, and Troy looked at the pair of men across from him. Haven sat in the huge chair with Phillip perched on the arm, both of them looking happy just to be near the other.

They made small talk about sports and such until Wally called them in to eat. Liam wheeled Jefferson up to the table to join them. He'd spent much of their discussion asleep in his chair, but Troy figured he just wanted to be around everyone—he knew *he* would in Jefferson's place. Another couple came in as they sat down, taking the empty places at the table. Wally introduced Troy to Mario and David. The conversation around the table centered mostly on ranch business, things like the chores for tomorrow and plans for the next few weeks.

"When will Dakota be back?" David asked between bites of Wally's amazingly rich scalloped potatoes.

"Not for two more weeks, and that's if he's lucky. He's supposed to have that weekend off, but they've often changed the schedule on him." Wally sat near Dakota's father and helped him eat slowly. It wasn't the cleanest affair, but no one else seemed to mind, so Troy was careful not to stare. Mostly, though, Jefferson sat and watched everyone without saying much, but he seemed happy as far as Troy could see.

After eating, everyone went back into the living room to continue talking. Mario and David excused themselves, saying they had chores to do, and Wally did the same, wheeling Jefferson down to his room.

"I should get going. It's a pain to take the track to the cabin in the dark," Troy said.

"I'll walk you out," Liam offered. Wally came back in the room, and Troy thanked him, saying good night before walking outside and across the yard to his truck, keenly aware of where Liam was the entire time. "It must be lonely at your cabin," Liam commented as Troy opened the door to his old truck.

"It is, sometimes," Troy admitted. Actually, he was finding it lonely most of the time, but he didn't want to appear whiny. Troy noticed Liam looking at him intensely, like he was waiting for him to say something or do something. "Um, I should get going," Troy stammered, flummoxed by Liam's expression and the intensity of his eyes. "Thank you for showing me around." Liam stepped back as Troy got in the truck and closed the door. Starting the engine, Troy switched on the headlights and turned the truck around. As he did, he saw the pack of dogs squirming around Liam's legs, jumping and vying for his attention. Liam picked up one of the small dogs, and Troy saw Liam getting multiple puppy kisses. He knew he'd be seeing that image in his mind for a long time.

Chapter Three

"YOU like him, don't you?" Phillip teased almost as soon as Liam got back in the house.

"Leave him alone," Wally said lightly, coming to Liam's defense. "Could you make sure all the cats are settled for the night? I just got a call, and it looks like it could be a long one."

Liam assented and watched as Wally hurried out the front door, and soon the taillights of his truck shone through the front window.

"But you do like him," Phillip persisted, and Liam saw Haven nudge him in the side.

"Be nice. Liam doesn't need any of your matchmaking, and if he likes Troy, it's none of your business." Liam saw Haven's gaze shift to him with a small smile. "Go on and take care of the cats. I have some things to do, and so does Phillip." Haven got up and left, with Phillip following not far behind. Liam breathed a sigh of relief as they left. He wasn't sure what he was feeling, but he didn't want to talk about it. He wasn't sure Troy was interested in him, but whenever the man looked at him, his heart sped up and his head got all floaty. He'd felt the rush of excitement a few times, but before it was always accompanied by his own doubts and fears. This time he knew Troy was gay, and maybe he was fixating on him just because he was gay and unattached. Liam didn't have enough experience to really know for sure. He sort of wanted to ask Wally, and maybe he would tomorrow.

Leaving by the back door, Liam grabbed a flashlight as he walked across the yard in the last light of the day. The cats were prowling their enclosures, becoming active after their day of lounging and sleeping in the shade. Liam checked to make sure each of them had water. They'd already eaten, so they should be fine for the night. As Liam approached Manny's enclosure, the impressively large cat stretched and ambled near him before sitting down to watch, cocking his head almost knowingly.

"Did you like Troy?" Manny stretched and seemed to be listening to him. "I suppose since you didn't attack the cage when he was here, at least you didn't hate him." Manny continued looking at him, and after another good stretch, Manny sat on the grass in front of him, gold eyes blinking. Manny had a habit of doing this sometimes, and Liam always wondered if Manny was trying to determine if he'd make a tasty snack.

A snarl from behind him followed by a low menacing growl reminded Liam that he was getting close to Shahrazad's enclosure. The tiger snarled again, and Liam jumped slightly, and then cried out as Manny let loose with a roar. That sound always startled Liam, and when he turned around, Manny was standing up on all four legs, looking every bit the king of the beasts. Shahrazad turned and walked away. Liam swore he saw an "I still got it" glint in Manny's eyes.

"Is everything okay?" Liam heard Wally ask as he approached. "What got into Manny?"

"Shahrazad was getting feisty, and he put her in her place," Liam answered. "That was a fast call."

"By the time I got there, the colt had been born and was standing. New horse owners always forget that horses have been giving birth for millennia without human intervention, but they always insist on calling the vet. So I checked out the colt, gave the owner the bill for the call, and left. Is everything okay here?"

"Seems to be. I was just having a talk with Manny," Liam confessed, to explain why he was lingering. Liam had always loved animals; they didn't judge and they accepted you as you were.

"And what were you talking about, man to ferocious beast?" Wally was teasing him a little. "It wouldn't have anything to do with a certain person living in a certain cabin, would it? It's okay. I saw how you were looking at each other, and that's fine. Just be careful, and know you don't have to rush into anything. There's a lot of hurt and pain in Troy's past."

Liam scrunched his eyebrows even though Wally probably couldn't really see it in the near dark. "How do you know?"

"Because he has the same look you sometimes get when something reminds you of the past. Just remember that it's okay to put yourself first and to protect your own heart. You can't lock it away, but you should be careful. All in all, I don't think Troy's a bad guy or anything, but he has a lot of issues he needs to work through. And I think there's a substantial reason why he's living alone in a cabin that's remote even by our standards." Liam heard Wally yawn. "Come on, we should get inside and leave the cats to their prowling. The sun comes up awfully early, and you know these babies let us know if we're late for breakfast."

"Yeah, I suppose they do." Liam walked toward the house as the last of the sunlight faded away.

THE following morning, Liam yawned repeatedly as he dressed and cleaned up in preparation for the day. Without waiting for breakfast, Liam went right to the refrigerator where Wally kept the meat for the cats and got their breakfast ready before carrying the metal pans out toward the enclosures. The cats were all alert and waiting for him, tongues licking, eyes focused on him. Liam did as Wally had shown him and carefully placed each portion of meat through the protected chutes, making sure they each had water before heading in for his own breakfast.

"I'm heading into town to pick up supplies," Haven said to Liam over a huge breakfast. "I was wondering if you'd ride in with me. I could use some help, and the other hands are out with the herds."

"Sure," Liam answered after swallowing his bacon. "How long will I be gone? I need to be back in time to check on the cats this afternoon." He also had other things that Wally had asked him to do, and he didn't want to let the man down.

"We'll be back before lunch," Haven said, and Liam looked to Wally, who nodded and smiled. Liam finished eating and was ready to go when Haven was. They didn't talk about much on their ride into town, and after stopping at the feed store to place an order, they made a stop at the hardware store, where Liam helped Haven load fence posts and other supplies. "I need to go to the bank, and then we can head back."

Liam nodded as he climbed into the truck, grateful for the rest after loading the heavy supplies. Haven parked in front of the bank building, and they walked inside. Liam noticed that Haven hung back a little until a middle-aged teller was free, and then he sidled up to the counter.

"Morning, Edie," Haven said with a wink, and Liam saw her smile brightly back at him. "I need to make a deposit." He handed her the slip, leaning on the counter. "How have you been?" Even Liam could see Haven was flirting with her.

"I'm good, darlin', how are you?"

"I'm really good," Haven responded.

"Did you hear the news?" she added cheerfully. "The community center is going to be built." She then looked around in that way all gossipers do, and Liam walked to one of the chairs in the lobby to wait. He didn't need to be eavesdropping on Haven's conversation. He figured Haven might be after the information he'd talked about last night, and Liam thought he would just be in the way. Liam waited until Haven had finished and saw him give Edie another wink and a smile before walking toward the door.

Haven's smile lasted until they reached the door and then it slid from his face, replaced by lines of deep worry. Haven said nothing, and Liam didn't ask, figuring it was none of his business. The ride back to the ranch was silent. Haven gripped the steering wheel so tight almost his entire hand was white by the time they pulled into the ranch drive. The truck had barely stopped before Haven had the engine off and was out the door, striding toward the house. Thinking whatever was going on wasn't his business, Liam began unloading the supplies.

"Do you need a hand?" Mario's partner, David, asked as Liam lowered the tailgate.

"Yes, please," Liam answered with relief. He hadn't been sure where most of the things went. David showed him, and together they began unloading the truck.

"Was that Haven stalking into the house?" David asked as they each carefully carried rolls of barbed wire into the equipment shed.

"Yeah," Liam answered.

"I take it he didn't get good news."

Liam nodded. "Don't know what it is, though. Probably none of my business." Regardless of what he said, Liam couldn't help being curious about what was going on. Eventually, once the truck was nearly empty, Haven came back out, and after saying a quick thank you, fired up one of the ATVs and took off across the range. Liam watched him go before finishing unloading the truck. Once everything was put away, Liam thanked David for his help and made his way to the back of the barn where Wally had an office, and got to work on the list of chores Wally had left for him.

Liam didn't see Haven for the rest of the day, and at lunch Wally seemed unusually quiet. Liam wanted to ask if there was anything he could do to help, but kept his mouth shut. He ate in near silence and then went back to work.

In the late afternoon, he ran the hose out near the enclosures, and after letting Shahrazad into the exercise area, he cleaned out her enclosure. He'd found out by accident that Manny loved the water, so when he was done, Liam pointed the hose at Manny and they played "bite the water" for a while. Manny was soaked by the time they were done, and when Liam turned away, Manny shook, and then it was Liam's turn to get wet.

By the time he'd finished rolling up the long hose, the warm sun had nearly dried him off, and he went inside to see if Wally had anything else he needed done. As he closed the door behind him, Liam heard Wally's voice drift in from the office. "I understand, Dakota. But I don't know what to do. I'm still a stranger here. No one is going to listen to me, even if I have helped half of them over the years." Liam opened the refrigerator and poured himself a glass of iced tea. "Haven is just as upset as you are. He took off on one of the ATVs a few hours ago and hasn't been back. I'd hate to be the steer that gets in his way."

Liam sat at the table and tuned out Wally's conversation as best he could before finishing his drink and leaving the house again to give Wally some privacy. Since he'd finished his chores, he was going to ask if anyone else needed any help, but no one was around but Wally, and Liam figured it best if he stayed out of the way. Walking around to the back, Liam wandered out onto the lawn, sitting in one of the chairs set beneath a young tree. His gaze went to the hills, where he knew Troy's cabin had to be located. He could see nothing of the building, and while he thought he might be able to see where the clearing was, he wasn't really sure.

Phillip's voice startled him. "Is there something interesting?"

Liam's head whirled toward the sound. "No, just looking."

"You know, it's okay to like him, and it's all right if he knows you like him. This isn't high school or a place where you need to size each other up. This is a safe place, and no one is going to bother you," Phillip told him, and Liam shrugged. "You know he's gay, and probably interested as well. At least he appeared that way from the look he was giving you."

"So what do I do?" Liam asked, pleased that he hadn't been imagining things.

"It's okay to ask him," Phillip said with a grin and a twitch of his eyebrows.

Liam felt like a dope for not thinking of that himself. "Was there something you needed?" Liam asked, changing the subject.

"Nice segue," Phillip quipped, and then he added, "I was wondering if you'd seen Haven. He's been out for a while, and I tried to call, but he isn't answering."

"He left pretty upset after we got back from town. We stopped at the bank, and he talked to that Tele-Edie person, and afterward he was pretty mad. Last I saw him, he was taking off on an ATV after talking to Wally. That's all I know, honest," Liam added when he saw the worried look on Phillip's face. Phillip nodded and left, leaving Liam alone with his thoughts. Everyone had advice about him and Troy, not that there was really a "him and Troy," but Liam wondered if it could be that easy. He knew Troy was gay, so it wasn't like he was going to get punched in the nose or anything. Going back inside, Liam found Wally still talking on the phone, so instead of interrupting, he set a note on the kitchen table and left the house. Liam hoped it was okay, but since he couldn't find anyone to ask, he put another note in the equipment shed before taking an ATV and heading down the driveway.

Liam took the now familiar route down the road and then up the hill to Troy's cabin. He made sure to make plenty of noise before rounding the small bend and parking at the edge of the clearing. Turning off the engine, Liam noticed just how quiet it was as the last echoes faded away with nothing to replace them. He got off the vehicle and took off his helmet. "Troy," Liam called but heard no answer. Slowly, he walked toward the cabin. The door was closed, but Troy's truck was parked next to the building. Troy couldn't have gone far, so he figured he'd wait a few minutes. "Troy?"

A few minutes turned into several more, and Liam figured he might as well leave. Walking back toward the ATV, Liam got on and started the engine. Turning around, Liam felt a little disappointed, but remembered that Troy wasn't expecting him. Liam knew he couldn't just expect the man to be waiting around in case he decided to visit.

Slowly, Liam rode to the edge of the clearing before starting the descent down the track. Reaching the first small curve, he noticed the underbrush at the edge of the track seemed as if it had been disturbed.

Liam didn't know what told him to stop, but he did and peered into the underbrush and saw that the land fell away from the track. He also saw that the ground was disturbed heading away from the track. "Troy." Liam wasn't sure what was going on, if anything. "Are you down there?"

Liam heard nothing and could see nothing. He was about to leave when he heard the slightest rustle. He thought it might have been an animal in the undergrowth and was about to get back on the ATV when he heard the sound again, coming from the same spot. Gingerly, Liam moved to the edge of the slope, holding onto saplings as he tried to keep his footing. "Troy," Liam called as he inched his way lower. Thick green leaves surrounded him, and Liam tried to keep his cool as he headed lower and lower into the ravine, stopping every few minutes to call and listen. A few times he heard the rustling sound, and he continued heading for it. Liam expected to see Troy lying on the ground at any time, hurt or worse. The rustling sound came again, and Liam saw it was two branches rubbing together in the slight breeze, nothing more.

Feeling like a fool, Liam turned around and began climbing back up, holding onto anything he could to give him extra purchase. Grabbing a sapling. He used his arms and legs to thrust himself upward as the small tree came out of the ground in his hand. Liam tried to keep himself from tumbling backward and instead ended up falling forward and sliding down the hill. He tried to stop himself, but every second he gained speed. Liam finally managed to stop himself when his feet encountered a boulder.

Liam rested, panting, facedown on the ground as he took inventory. He seemed to be okay, but then his leg began to throb. Liam rolled over, thankfully not seeing any blood, but his leg hurt like hell when he put much weight on it. He probably could have walked on level ground, but there was no way he was going to be able to climb the hill.

"Is anyone there?" Liam called, knowing full well it was unlikely that anyone would hear him. Troy wasn't around, as he'd found out earlier. At least he'd left notes about where he'd gone, so eventually someone would come looking for him and would see the ATV. Liam shifted to try to get comfortable and his leg throbbed painfully, but he managed to get himself into a seated position with his legs in front of him, and if he sat still, the throbbing diminished to a dull ache.

Liam lost track of time as he sat and listened for any signs of activity, but he heard nothing but the sound of the wind through the trees. Liam figured he should be grateful he was in the shade and that it wasn't raining. As soon as the thought crossed his mind, he actually looked toward the sky just to make sure he hadn't jinxed himself. "Hello," someone called from the track above him; Liam thought it sounded like Troy.

"I'm down here," he called, grateful that someone had found him.

"Liam, is that you? What are you doing down there?" Troy's voice drifted through the trees.

"It's a long story." Liam felt like a complete idiot. "I hurt my leg, and I can't climb back up." Liam shifted so he could look up the hill, and his leg began throbbing again.

"I'll be right back," Troy told him, and then all was quiet once again. Liam listened and waited. After a while, he heard someone coming down the hill, the underbrush crunching, and he heard cursing that got louder and louder.

"I'm sorry, Troy," Liam said as Troy got close.

"What made you come down here?" Troy asked with an edge to his voice.

Liam turned his head toward where Troy stood near him, holding a rope that wound up the hill. "I thought you might have fallen." Liam knew he must look like a complete dope, and he looked down at his legs. "There was a slide near the top, and I heard movement down here, and I thought it might have been you. Then I fell, and my leg hurt too much to get back up." Liam glanced at Troy and saw a surprised look on his face.

"You came down here for me?" Troy asked as he knelt near where Liam sat.

"I thought you might have been hurt. It really sounded like a person was trying to get my attention. I thought I was going to rescue you, but instead I ended up stuck here." Liam was angry at himself for being such a fool. He should have just gotten help.

"That's the nicest thing anyone has done for me in a long time," Troy told him with a huge smile. "Can you stand at all? I can probably help you get up the hill." Liam gingerly got up, doing his best to keep his balance on the steep slope. He could put some weight on his leg, but looking toward the top, Liam couldn't figure out how they were going to make it to the road. Troy put an arm around his waist, supporting a lot of his weight. "Just take it easy. The slope isn't as steep a little ways over, so we're going to move in the direction of the cabin, and we should have an easier time."

"I'll try," Liam agreed, liking the feel of Troy's arm around him.

Slowly they moved along the slope, every step on his leg painful, but Liam found that with Troy's help he could move. Troy played out more rope as they went, and sure enough, the slope evened out and they began to move forward and upward. It took a while, but together they were finally able to reach the track at the top of the slope. Liam's ATV was some distance away, and Troy settled him on the ground before retrieving it. "Carefully get on behind me, and I'll drive you to the cabin."

Liam held on, balancing mostly on his good leg for the slow ride to the cabin. Once Troy turned off the engine, he helped Liam inside and onto the bed. "Let me take a look at your leg," Troy said, and Liam nodded as he felt warm hands slide under his pant leg. Liam shivered and the pain receded as Troy's gentle touch took precedence over the pain. "There doesn't seem to be anything broken. But you have a nasty bruise, and your leg is already swelling. I should probably get you back to the ranch, and you should have a doctor look at it just to make sure there isn't something else wrong," Troy told him. Liam noticed that Troy wasn't moving his hand, and all his attention focused on where Troy's hand met his skin.

"What?" Liam asked, not having understood a word.

"Let's get you back to the ranch," Troy said with an indulgent smile. "I'll take you down in the truck. I'm sure someone can arrange to pick up the ATV."

"I suppose," Liam answered as Troy slipped his hand away from his leg.

"Was there something important you came up here to tell me?" Troy asked as he helped Liam to his feet, strong arms around his waist once again.

Liam wasn't sure he should say anything now. But he'd come all this way and nearly gotten himself killed. Okay, maybe that was exaggerating a little. He just wasn't quite sure how to ask what he wanted to ask, so Liam turned toward Troy and kissed him. It didn't last long, and when Liam pulled back, the shocked, openmouthed look on Troy's face told him all he needed to know. "I'm sorry," Liam said, feeling like a total fool. After all, what had he expected—a single quick kiss and then Troy would be declaring his eternal love?

"Hey, there's nothing to be sorry for. I just don't know why you did that," Troy said with obvious confusion in his voice, and Liam turned away, not willing to face Troy's rejection.

"I like you, and I wasn't sure how to tell you, so I thought…." Liam's words trailed off, and he hobbled toward the door, moving out of Troy's arms. "I know it was stupid. I shouldn't have done anything."

"Hey. It wasn't stupid. In fact, it was rather nice."

"Then why are you acting like a butthead?" Liam asked, hearing some of his hurt in his own voice. Liam leaned against the door to get his balance. He wished he could walk so he could simply get out of here and back to the ranch.

"I don't mean to be," Troy said as he stepped closer to Liam. "You need some help or you'll hurt your leg further, so let me get you to the truck."

Against his better judgment, Liam let Troy help him outside and into the passenger seat of the truck before closing the door. Liam watched as Troy walked around the front before getting in himself. "You didn't answer my question," Liam said, crossing his arms in front of his chest.

"Liam," Troy began, and Liam heard the condescending tone.

"You're not helping the 'acting like a butthead' thing."

Troy sighed and started the truck. "I guess I'm wondering what you could possibly see in me, okay? As you said, I act like a butthead, and the people in my life tend to get hurt. I'm not going to be very good for you or anyone else." Troy backed the truck up before turning around in the clearing.

"You could have just said you didn't like me," Liam stated, and the truck braked to a halt.

"I never said I didn't like you," Troy said, and Liam saw his head turn to look at him. "I do like you, and that's the problem. I shouldn't. I shouldn't like anyone that way, no matter how much I like them." Troy took a deep breath. "I don't deserve to be around anyone I care about, and if you care about me, you'll only get hurt, just like them." Liam could see a tear run down Troy's face, and he saw him brush it away before steadying himself. "I'm not good for anyone, Liam."

"Why don't you let me judge what's best for me," Liam said weakly, and Troy stayed silent as they slowly descended the hill. "Fine, if you don't want to talk to me, that's just fine."

"It's for your own good," Troy responded halfheartedly. "Besides, what would a bright-eyed, adorably cute guy like you want with a guy like me, anyway? I have nothing to offer you except grief and heartache. You don't deserve either."

"How do you know what you can offer me or anyone, or what we need or want? So someone hurt you, and you feel bad about it. That's no reason to lock yourself away," Liam countered.

They reached the bottom of the hill, and the truck picked up speed. "Liam, I wasn't hurt by someone; I was the one who did the hurting. I had a wife and daughter and I hurt both of them very badly."

"But I thought you were gay—" Liam began, and he widened his eyes as he realized what Troy was saying. "You were married?" Troy nodded as he continued driving. "And they didn't know you were gay?" Liam watched as Troy shook his head.

"They do now because I told them. My wife cried for days, and neither she nor my daughter want to speak to me. Not that I can blame them. I lied to my wife for years." Troy pulled into the driveway of the ranch, pulling to a stop in front of the house. "So now you see. I hurt them, and I'll only hurt you too. So you're better off finding someone who deserves you and isn't going to disappoint you." Liam saw Troy reach across the seat and felt the tips of his fingers touch his cheek ever so softly. "You really are wonderful, you know that? You risked yourself because you thought I was hurt. But you did that for someone who, if he had fallen down that ravine, would probably be better off left there." Troy's fingers slipped away, and Liam saw the front door open. Wally rushed out, and Liam opened the truck door, carefully getting out of the truck.

Wally hurried over to him and must have seen he was hurting, because he helped him walk toward the house. "What happened?" Wally asked, looking back toward the truck.

"I fell down a hill," Liam answered succinctly, feeling as though his heart was hurting. He had no idea why. He'd only met Troy a few days ago, and they hadn't spent that much time together, but as he heard Troy's truck drive away, Liam felt as though something potentially special was leaving as well.

"What were you doing there?" Wally inquired. "I saw your notes and was starting to get worried when I saw him drive up."

"I'll be fine, Wally. I hurt my leg and my pride." He'd gotten his heart hurt as well, but he wasn't going to tell Wally that. He was a fool, and he'd let himself get carried away. He knew he shouldn't have.

Wally helped him inside and onto the sofa. "Get your pants off so I can take a look at your leg."

"It'll be fine," Liam countered, but all he got was a stern look that didn't abate until Liam did as Wally asked and slowly slid off his jeans.

"That's one hell of a bruise, and it probably goes all the way to the bone." Liam felt Wally's hands on his skin, but they didn't feel anything like Troy's had. They were gentle and caring, but nothing more. "I'll get a cold compress. That should help with some of the swelling, and I'll get you something for pain. You're dang lucky you didn't break anything."

"I know," Liam said. "Thank you for helping."

"How did you fall down a ravine?" Wally asked once he returned, and Liam hissed as the cold of the compress touched his skin.

"I didn't fall. I climbed down," Liam explained, making the noise again as the muscles in his leg contracted from the cold. "I thought Troy might have been hurt." Liam didn't explain further, and thankfully Wally didn't press it, but he did huff softly and give Liam a suspicious look.

"Dinner will be ready in a little while," Wally informed Liam once he was settled. Wally left, and Liam heard him working in the kitchen, banging and making enough noise to wake the dead. Something was definitely bothering Wally, and Liam had the feeling that it wasn't about him—at least that's what he hoped.

"Are you mad at me?" Liam asked, and the banging stopped abruptly.

"No. Not at all," Wally answered, poking his head around the corner and forcing a smile. He didn't elaborate, and while Liam was dying to know what had Wally so upset, the pain in his leg and the sting from Troy's rejection kept his mind occupied.

Chapter Four

"WHAT do you need?" Kevin asked suspiciously when he answered Troy's call.

"It's good to talk to you too," Troy sniped, and he nearly hung up the phone, but his desperation and confusion stopped him.

"I've barely heard from you in months and now you call—it's a safe bet that you want something." Kevin didn't sound angry as much as guarded, and Troy had to admit, his brother's suspicions were probably well-founded. Not that he'd ever admit it to anyone. "Are you still at the cabin?"

"Yes," Troy answered.

"How much money do you need?" Kevin asked sounding resigned.

"I didn't call for anything like that." Damn, maybe he should just hang up and be done with it.

"Wait a minute. You're calling to actually talk to me? You don't want anything?" The tone of Kevin's voice was really starting to piss him off.

"Don't be a smartass," Troy retorted, wondering if making this call was a good idea, but he didn't know anyone else he could ask. "I called because I need your help, and before you ask, not that kind of help." *God, why was this so hard?* "I need some advice."

"You want my opinion?" Kevin asked. "On what?"

"I don't know anything about this gay stuff, and you do."

Kevin laughed. "Gay stuff? Come on, Troy. You still don't want to see yourself as gay, but you are. And if you can accept it, you'll be happier. Besides, it's not stuff, but part of who you are." He heard Kevin sigh. "What do you need?"

"I met someone who likes me, and I don't know what to do," Troy admitted.

Kevin was quiet for what seemed like a long time. "What do you want to do?"

"How in the hell should I know? Besides, I've probably already messed things up royally."

"Wait!" Kevin said firmly. "Just slow down and tell me what's going on."

Troy took a deep breath and explained about meeting Liam and what had happened.

"Okay," Kevin began once Troy was done, "you like this Liam."

"Yes. I told you I did."

"And he put himself in danger, injuring himself climbing down this hill because he thought you might be hurt?" Kevin didn't give him a chance to answer this time. "He also said he liked you and he kissed you. So what's the problem? You say this guy is adorable, and he's obviously selfless, he likes you, and you're calling me instead of being with him. What's holding you back?"

Troy swallowed hard and said nothing. "What if I'm not good enough for him?" There, he'd actually said it. All his life, regardless of how he truly felt, Troy'd had to at least look as though he were in charge, and letting that mask slip was much harder than he had expected.

"You're good enough for anyone. I know the years of hiding and then the fallout from telling Jeanie have done a number on your self-confidence and self-image, but you can't let that color the rest of your life. You're being honest with yourself and you're being honest with him, right?"

"Of course."

"Then you have nothing to worry about. You're still the same person you always were. You've always been a people person, and just because you're gay doesn't mean that should change. The old Troy is still you, you're just gay now and able to admit it."

"But what do I do?"

"What do you want to do? Do you like Liam?" All of Kevin's earlier impatience and suspicion were gone, and Troy heard a tone of voice from his brother he'd rarely heard before— compassion.

"Yes, I do." Troy couldn't help smiling as he remembered the excitement and energy in Liam's voice as he showed him the "kitties." "He's really something."

"Then since you asked my advice, I'll give it to you. I think you owe Liam an apology, and then you can pray like hell that he gives you a second chance."

"Is that all?" Troy said.

"If you like him, then you should decide if you like him enough to be honest with him. He deserves that. It's the honesty part that's hard. If you really like Liam, then you need to let him see the real you. Loving someone means letting them into your heart."

"But what if I get hurt, or what if I hurt him again?"

Kevin laughed. "When was the last time you worried about hurting anyone? You didn't worry about that all the years you were with Jeanie."

"That's not fair!" Troy cried into the phone.

"It may not be, but it's true. You've never worried about hurting anyone in the past, but you're worried about hurting Liam. He must really be something. Either that, or my brother has suddenly turned into a compassionate, caring human being." Kevin's teasing tone shot through the phone.

"Let's not go too far," Troy retorted, and Kevin laughed.

"Seriously, you've changed, and forgive me for sounding condescending, but I think it's for the better. You deserve to be happy. You always have. So go apologize to this Liam—and you better make it a good one, because he sounds pretty amazing. By the way, how long have you known him?"

"A little over a week, I guess." Troy explained how they met at gunpoint and had Kevin laughing.

"That settles it. If this guy can tell you he likes you after you pointed a gun at him, he's something special and you need to tell him that. He deserves to know how you truly feel about him. I will warn you, there's the very real possibility that he'll tell you to take a hike."

"That's what I'm afraid of."

"So put on your big-girl panties and suck it up. If anything could possibly help you get Liam's attention, it's being honest with him. If you care about him, you need to tell him and not worry about how it makes you look, or your own ego."

"Thanks." Troy tried to sound casual, but that last remark got under his skin.

"Don't mention it. Now let the groveling begin." Kevin laughed lightly. "And be sure to let me know what happens." Kevin hung up, and Troy shoved his phone in his pocket. Kevin was right—he really did owe Liam an apology and some honesty, and there was no time like the present. Leaving the cabin, Troy got into his truck and drove back toward the ranch, hoping to heaven Wally wasn't waiting for him with a shotgun.

Troy parked next to the other trucks in the ranch driveway and walked toward the door. The dogs seemed to be occupied with bones and barely looked up from the grass as they chewed. Climbing the stairs, Troy knocked on the door and waited for it to open.

"You know, I should beat the crap out of you," Wally told him as soon as he opened the door. "Just when I think you aren't so bad, you turn into a complete and total shit."

"I know," Troy agreed, and he saw Wally's eyes widen in surprise. "I don't have an excuse except that I'm an idiot. Do you think I could talk to Liam?"

Wally's eyebrows narrowed. "I'll see if he wants to see you." The door closed, and Troy found himself staring at wood. Troy waited and waited and was about to leave when the door opened again and Wally stepped back to let Troy inside.

Liam was lying on the sofa with his leg up and a cold pack on it, his eyes filled with hurt, and Troy knew it wasn't just because of the pain in his leg. Troy knew most of the sadness in Liam's eyes was because of him. "Do you want me to stay?" Wally asked Liam as he stared daggers at Troy.

"No, I'll be fine," Liam answered as he gingerly wedged himself into a seated position. "I don't think Troy is going to pull a shotgun on me this time." For a second Troy thought that might have been Liam's attempt at humor, but he realized it wasn't. Liam was reminding him of his repeated bad behavior, and he had no argument for it. Wally left the room, but it was obvious that he was staying nearby. "What do you want?"

Troy shifted from foot to foot, wondering just how to say what he wanted to say. "I wanted to make sure you were okay. I should have seen you into the house when I was here before."

Liam's gaze hardened. "You've seen me, and my leg is swollen and hurting. Now you know and you can go."

Troy didn't know what to say and nearly turned to leave, but he'd come this far, so he figured he would go for broke. "I'm sorry, Liam. I shouldn't have pushed you away like that. What you tried to do for me was pretty special, and I shouldn't have acted like that. You deserve to be treated better than that." Troy wasn't sure he was saying it right. "I liked it when you kissed me, and I liked it when I had my arms around you."

"Then why did you act like a butthead?"

"Because I was scared, I guess," Troy admitted.

"You were scared of me." Liam's voice clearly conveyed his skepticism. "The guy you pulled a gun on the first time we met?" So they were back to that again.

"You're never going to let me forget that, are you?" Troy tried to make light of it, but Liam was having none of it.

"Why should I?"

"Because I came here to apologize and tell you I was wrong. I shouldn't have pushed you away. What I told you was true. I didn't think I was good enough for you. Hell, I still don't, but then I'm finding that I really don't know crap about very much."

"So why the change of heart?" Troy thought he caught a slight thaw in Liam's tone.

"I talked to my brother, and he told me I was a fool. I'd already figured that part out before I called him. I think I just needed to hear it, though, and Kevin didn't mince words."

"You said he was the smart one." There was a definite note of teasing in Liam's words, and Troy felt himself begin to hope just a little.

"I did, didn't I?" Troy smiled slightly before kneeling next to the sofa. "The truth is that I came back because you're a sweet man who put himself in danger because you thought I was hurt. I may not deserve you, but I certainly should not have hurt you." Troy took a chance and placed Liam's hand in his. "I'm sorry for thinking I knew what was best for you. I should have known I didn't since I barely know what's best for me." Troy had no idea what to expect—he'd never made a declaration like that to anyone before. A lifetime of hiding who he was and guarding his feelings had left him unsure of his own or anyone else's. Then Liam smiled at him. Granted, it was small and tentative, but Troy felt as though his world had awakened from a long night's sleep, almost like he'd been asleep his entire life and now the sun had come out in that small smile. "I really do like you, Liam, and I'm sorry I hurt you."

Liam scooted over on the sofa and patted the cushion lightly. Troy got up and gingerly perched on the edge of the cushion, not wanting to hurt Liam. "You said you were married."

Troy nodded slowly. He knew he needed to tell Liam the story, and he figured he should get it over with. Kevin had, in essence, told him to stop hiding and be honest. "My first marriage to Mary didn't last very long, and about a year later I met and started dating Jeanie. We eventually got married, that was about six years ago, and shortly after, she became pregnant with Sofia."

"Did you know you were gay?"

"My brother Kevin has been out for years, even in high school, and I knew I had these feelings for other guys, but I hoped they would go away. After my first marriage failed, I should have examined my life. Looking back, I realize now that I was in complete denial. More than anything, I wanted to be normal, so I buried that part of myself because I wanted to have a normal life. After Sofia was born, it got easier for a long time because I loved her more than anything and I had her to live for and take care of."

"It sounds as though your life was perfect and you had everything you could have wanted," Liam said quietly. "What happened?"

"I was living a lie. For a number of years I was happy and contented. Then I met a guy at work, and we became friends and then more. It started out so innocently, but he saw through me, and we started messing around sometimes. After a while, he was transferred to another office, but I'd had a taste of what was missing." Troy was not at all proud of what he'd done, and he looked down at the floor, unable to look the sweet man in the eyes any longer. "Six months ago my brother was staying with us and he saw some text messages and confronted me. I hadn't been happy in a long time, and he made me realize I couldn't continue to lie to Jeanie. I waited a few days, until Sofia was at a friend's house, and I told her." Troy felt a lump grow in his throat. "It devastated her, Liam," Troy said softly, barely able to get the words out of his mouth. "She cried for hours and spent days in bed trying to retreat from the world. I loved her, I really did, and I hurt her so badly." Troy stood up and walked across the room, looking out the large window into the twilight. "In one day, I nearly destroyed the person I cared for most in the world. She deserved to know, she really did, but my refusal to see who I was and the lies I used to cover it up only added to her pain."

Troy stopped talking, focusing his eyes on nothing except his memory of the look on Jeanie's face.

"You did the right thing," Liam said softly from behind him.

"Did I?" Troy turned around. "Sometimes I think it would have been kinder to have said nothing, to simply have continued lying to her. And when I asked for a divorce, I think she could have gotten over it more easily if I could have come up with some excuse that wouldn't have made her feel as though the entire life we'd built together was nothing to me, because that's how she felt. I did love her, I always had, but by telling her like I did, I think I hurt her worse."

"She probably would have found out eventually, and that would have hurt her too," Liam observed quite accurately.

Troy shrugged. "I'd already covered up who I was for selfish reasons. I could have covered up a little longer to spare her feelings. But I've always been selfish and self-centered, and I thought honesty would be easier to take. I know now I was probably wrong." His family's devastation and the pained and hurt looks on all their faces came back to him in a rush of near agony. "After I told Jeanie, she insisted I move out of the house. After that, everything became a blur. In the divorce, I gave her nearly everything. She deserved it, for Sofia. I inherited some money from my parents and I turned all that over to her as well, so Jeanie would have enough money to raise Sofia."

"Have you seen either of them?"

"No. Jeanie insisted that I stay away from both of them, and I'd already hurt them enough that I didn't want to cause either of them pain. The last time I saw Sofia, she refused to speak with me for the longest time, and when she finally did speak, she told me she hated me because I made Mommy cry all the time." Troy felt tears run down his cheeks. "Those words hurt more than anything I've ever felt in my life. I thought of ending it all, but I couldn't do it. My life totally fell apart, and I lost my job shortly after the divorce. Not that I can blame them, either." Troy tried not to fall completely apart as he relived all the grief he'd caused everyone he'd once been close to.

Needing to bring this to an end, Troy told the last of it. "A few months ago, my uncle died and left my brother and me his estate, which included the cabin, and once I could, I came here. I'd hurt everyone in my life, so I figured the best thing I could do would be to go someplace where I couldn't injure anyone else. And I couldn't even keep from messing that up, because I hurt you."

"You were really married twice?" Liam asked, before adding, "and you actually have a daughter?"

Troy smiled as he fished into his pocket. "I do." He pulled out his cell phone and showed Liam a picture. "She's almost five, and as smart and funny as I could ever have hoped for." Troy's voice threatened to break again as he realized just how long it had been since he'd seen her. "Jeanie didn't want me seeing her after I came out to her, and I didn't argue. I thought it would be best for Sofia, but of all the mistakes I've made, that's been the biggest one. I've called a few times, and Jeanie has put her on the phone, but Sofia never says much, and I know she wonders what's going on. I have no idea what Jeanie has told her—she refuses to talk to me other than in the most distant way and then she put Sofia on the phone."

"Where is Sofia now? I mean, where does she live?" The look of pity on Liam's face was almost too much for Troy to take, and he turned back to the window. He hadn't told Liam this for his sympathy, although he had to face the fact that the story did make him look rather pathetic, and frankly, it was how he felt.

"She and Jeanie still live in the house we had together outside Baltimore. Regardless of how things worked out between us, Jeanie is a great mother, and she was a wonderful wife. I hope someday she'll be able to find someone to make her happy. She deserves that." Troy wandered back toward the sofa, watching the mixture of emotions on Liam's face.

"What do you feel you deserve?" Liam asked softly.

"Deserve? I don't deserve anything. I hurt them both and I should pay for that hurt for the rest of my life." Troy waited for Liam to agree with him and then he could simply get back in his truck and head back to the cabin, knowing at least he'd been honest with Liam and allowed him to make up his own mind.

"Dramatic much?" Liam asked, and Troy saw that ghost of a smile again. "Is that everything?"

Troy nodded slowly and watched as Liam seemed to move in slow motion, reaching his hand out to Troy's, and then sliding his fingers into his.

"You promise to tell me the truth?" Liam asked, and Troy nodded again. He'd already told Liam the worst things he'd ever done in his life.

"I promise, and I should give you some time to think about all this." Troy began to walk away, but Liam didn't let go of his hand and instead tugged him closer.

"It's a lot to digest," Liam said seriously before nervously biting his lower lip.

"I know it is, and I want you to understand that I under no circumstances hold it against you if it's too much for you to deal with. I'm just glad you were willing to listen." Troy squeezed Liam's hand and then let it go before walking toward the door. He turned to look at Liam resting on the sofa, his dark hair falling adorably into his eyes. It sounded sappy, even in his own mind, but he wanted to make sure he remembered Liam if this was the last time he saw him. Then he turned and opened the door. Stepping outside, Troy closed it behind him and went down the stairs, walking toward the truck. As he approached the truck, he heard the ranch house door open and footsteps rapidly descend the stairs.

"Listen to me," Wally began from behind him, not waiting for Troy to turn around. "If you're playing some sort of game, then you better end it now!" Wally was nearly shouting. "That young man in there cares for you. Why in the hell he does is beyond me, but he does. He's lying on that sofa with tears running down his cheeks because of that sob story you told him. Every word of that better be true, and you had better be willing to follow through when it comes to Liam."

Troy held up his hand. "I've never lied to him, not once. He's probably the one person I've been truly honest with about myself since I was in high school."

Some of the fire went out of Wally's eyes. "All I can say is, you had better. That man has been through more hell than you can imagine, and some of the things he's told me would curl even your hair. It most certainly would get you off this self-pity train you're on. Yes, you've had a hard time of things, but that was your own making and you need to take the consequences." Wally seemed to understand how he sounded, and his face softened further. "Sorry, that was condescending as hell, and I don't mean to sound that way. It's just that Liam's pain is not his own making, and he doesn't deserve any of it." Wally seemed to run out of steam as another truck pulled into the drive. It had barely stopped when Haven got out and raced toward Wally.

"There's a special town council meeting in a week," Haven said breathlessly. "They certainly aren't wasting any time trying to get this passed." He seemed to notice Troy and stopped sputtering.

"You two need to talk, but I can promise you, Wally, I don't intend to hurt Liam."

"We'll see," was Wally's only response before he turned to Haven, and the two of them walked into the house, with Haven already sputtering about water rights and pollution. Troy wondered what that was about for a few seconds, but thoughts of Liam pushed that aside, and looking toward the front window, Troy thought of Liam settled on the sofa just inside before getting in the truck and driving back to the cabin.

Troy made himself a very late dinner before settling outside the front door in his rustic chair, listening to the night. A few times, he could hear the sound of the sizable stream that flowed where the hill the cabin was on met the rangeland below. If he closed his eyes, he could almost see the spot where he'd been fishing. Troy wondered if Liam liked to fish. No matter what he did, his mind kept wandering to Liam and the way he'd unselfishly thought he was coming to Troy's rescue, and the way Troy had rewarded him with hurt. If Liam gave him another chance, Troy was determined to make good on it. Troy settled back in his chair and decided not to fight his thoughts, and images of Liam hurt and on the sofa filled his mind, followed by the way Liam had looked while he was showing him the cats. The man was beautiful, there was no doubt about that, but his beauty radiated from inside, and that was what Troy could not get out of his head. Liam's blue eyes shone not just because they were as deep as the sea, but because of the man behind them.

The sky darkened and fireflies sparked in the trees around him. If Liam wasn't injured, Troy would have liked nothing better than to share this with him. Did he deserve that? Probably not, but he did want it, more than anything he could remember, except maybe the way he wanted to see his daughter again. Sighing to himself, Troy let night fall around him, his head resting against the back of his chair. He lost track of time and began to drift off. Jerking awake as the cool air settled around him, Troy shivered before getting up and going inside. After cleaning up, he climbed into bed and closed his eyes.

THE next thing he remembered were voices outside his cabin and light shining through the windows. The voices didn't sound familiar. Getting out of bed, Troy pulled on a pair of jeans and a sweatshirt before slipping on a pair of shoes.

"This isn't supposed to be here, according to the map, but we passed over a large stream on our way up here that could solve our water problems if the council turns us down," Troy heard a man's voice say, and another shushed him. Opening his door, he saw two men looking like they were about to knock. They were dressed in jeans and collared shirts with new shoes, like they didn't usually work outside of an office and were spending a day in the field. One of them held a large map in his hands.

"Can I help you?" Troy asked suspiciously, wondering if he should have remembered his gun.

"There seems to be something wrong. Our company has leased this land from the federal government and this cabin isn't supposed to be here." The men seemed genuinely confused, and the one consulted the map again.

"I don't know what you think you've leased, but the cabin and the land belong to my brother and me," Troy said levelly, his curiosity piqued. "Do you mind if I look at that map?" The man moved around, and Troy saw the map with a large area marked in red. "Is this the area you leased?"

"Yes."

Troy nodded and pointed toward the road to the cabin. "This is the road you came up here on, and you can see it's well outside the area you're leasing. I think you got yourself confused. If you go back down and turn at the main road, you'll probably need to head west about four miles and you should come to this road here. That should lead you back toward the land you have marked. I've never been back there, but you should be able to find your way from there. If you don't mind my asking, what did you lease the land for?" Troy knew from the map that the land they'd circled was mostly high hills and low mountains.

"Thank you very much for your help," the man with the map said, evading Troy's question.

He didn't press them, and watched as they got in their truck and carefully turned around and headed down the hill. Troy noticed from the out-of-state plates that it was probably a rental, but the snippet of conversation he'd heard was enough to make him wonder. Going back inside, Troy made breakfast before starting his chores, but his mind kept switching from the behavior of his morning visitors to Liam. Once he'd finished the few chores he needed to do, Troy couldn't stand it anymore, so he got in the truck and wove his way down the track. He pulled into the ranch driveway and got out of the truck, surprised to see Liam standing on the front porch. "Shouldn't you be inside resting your leg?" Liam looked a little wobbly, and Troy was concerned he was about to fall over.

"I couldn't stand lying around all day," Liam explained as Troy approached. "My leg doesn't hurt like it did yesterday, although it's turned all kinds of colors."

"You should get inside before Wally sees you."

Liam grinned, and Troy felt his heart pull him forward. "He is a bit of a mother hen. But he's off with Haven worrying about something. I heard Haven say something about water rights and the town, but I don't really know what's gotten into both of them. Wally's been nervous, and Haven's been as grumpy as a bear." Troy saw Liam look toward the road and then turn to go inside as a truck pulled into the driveway.

"Was that Liam I saw going in the house?" Wally asked, or more accurately, demanded, as he walked toward the porch. Troy kept quiet and followed Wally inside. Liam was back on the sofa, resting quietly, but Troy noticed the mischief in his eyes. Wally did as well, because he glared at Liam before moving on to the kitchen. Haven came in then, following Wally through.

"We can't let these people get away with this. They're trying to buy the town's support," Haven said indignantly.

Troy jumped when Haven's fist banged the table.

"Calm down. I agree with you, but I don't know what we can do until the council meeting," Wally explained in a calm voice.

Bells went off in Troy's head as something clicked into place.

"What is this meeting about?" Troy asked, not sure he should interrupt.

"Someone's leased up a large tract of land, and they want the town to lease them some of their water rights. The company and the council are being very secretive about what they want. All we've got to go on is rumor because no one who knows is really talking," Haven said as Wally placed a mug of coffee on the table.

"I think I might be able to help." Troy explained about his visitors that morning and about the map they'd shown him. "They were obviously guys who'd spent more time in an office than the field. They thought my cabin was on the land they'd leased, and they seemed interested in the trout stream that borders my property and yours." Troy sat next to Liam, sharing smiles back and forth. Troy saw Haven pick up his mug and carry it into the living room, sitting in the chair across from them.

"Are you two…?" Haven asked, making a motion back and forth with his hand.

"Haven, stay on the subject," Wally said before turning to Troy. "Can you tell from the map what they might want?"

"I think it's mining of some type. The land they've leased is all vertical, with a road leading into it, and I suspect they're looking for something. It isn't for farming or ranching, that's for sure, and mining requires a steady source of water, which is probably why they want the rights from the town. The map didn't show any water source as far as I could see, other than the river."

"And all those rights are apportioned," Haven supplied. "Wonderful. Miners will come in, steal our water, rip the hills apart, and pollute the land to no end." He sighed loudly. "At least we know what we're up against, not that it helps us all that much." Haven groused a little more before taking his mug to the sink and disappearing down the hall, where Troy heard soft talking. Wally went back in the kitchen, leaving them alone, and Troy figured this was the moment of truth.

"Did you sleep okay last night?" Troy asked, figuring that Liam probably had a pretty rough night.

"Not really. I kept thinking of you and wondering what you were doing," Liam admitted, and Troy felt the intensity in Liam's gaze as their eyes met.

"I sat outside my door wondering the same thing about you." God, he knew they sounded a little lame, but Troy didn't really care. It appeared that Liam was willing to accept him, even knowing his past and his mistakes. "I hoped you were okay as I sat watching the lightning bugs. By the way, I wanted to ask if you like fishing. I found this great stream at the base of the hill. I've been fishing there a few times, and I was wondering if you'd like to come fishing with me when your leg feels better."

Sadness skittered over Liam's face for a split second, and then it was gone. "I used to go fishing all the time, but I haven't since I left home." Troy watched as Liam seemed to debate whether he wanted to say anything more. "I'd like to go fishing with you. Maybe in a few days I'll be able to stand more, and my leg should be feeling better by then." Liam smiled, and Troy couldn't help himself. He moved to where Liam had propped himself and tentatively edged closer. Liam didn't pull away, and Troy asked permission with his eyes before lightly pressing his lips to Liam's. As kisses went, it probably wasn't the smoothest or done with the most finesse, but to Troy it seemed like the best kiss in the world.

"Is that what I've been missing?" Troy asked when he pulled back enough to see Liam's smile before kissing him again. Troy had to know if the zing that went up his spine and the urge to pull Liam closer weren't flukes, and they weren't. It felt almost like someone was shooting small electric currents through him, and Troy never wanted to stop. "Wow," Troy said softly when they broke the kiss once again, and this time he was the one smiling like an idiot.

"It's never been like that for me either," Liam admitted as they simply looked at each other and smiled.

"Okay, you two Cheshire cats, I have work to do, and Liam needs his rest. Troy, come on back for dinner, and you two can look at each other longingly again," Wally said as he hurried into the room. "The nurse will be bringing Jefferson out, so you can keep each other company. I have some appointments, and I'll probably be back late this afternoon."

Troy stole another kiss before Wally shooed him out of the house, and Troy drove back up the hill, his heart leaping and his spirit worlds lighter.

Chapter Five

LIAM was going completely and totally stir-crazy. For two days, every time Liam looked like he was about to get onto his feet, Wally was there to scold him. Troy had visited every day, and he and Wally seemed to have worked out a truce. Pushing back the covers, Liam got out of bed as quietly as he could and walked to the bathroom, checking how his leg felt. It was still sore and definitely stiff, but a lot of the pain was gone, and Liam was determined to get back to work. He'd slacked off long enough, and Wally had had to do his chores, which did not sit well with Liam at all.

"Where do you think you're going?" Wally asked him as soon as Liam stepped out of the bathroom again.

"I'm getting dressed and going to work. I promise not to overdo it, but I need to do something or the cats are going to forget all about me." Liam returned Wally's stern look. This time, he wasn't backing down. "Besides, I'm not letting you do my work anymore."

Wally's expression softened. "As long as you rest when you need to."

"I promise, Mama Wally," Liam said before jerking back as Wally took a light swat at him.

"Come on and eat, and then you can feed the beasts," Wally told him before heading back toward the kitchen, and Liam got dressed before walking carefully toward the kitchen. His leg felt okay, and after breakfast, Liam went to the refrigerator, got the meat for the cats, and happily walked out the back door and across the yard to the pens.

"Did you miss me?" Liam asked, and Manny yawned once before Liam dropped his food into the enclosure. Shahrazad took a swipe at him, and the others were pretty much just interested in their food. "Yup, everything's normal."

"You look like you're feeling better." Troy's voice drifted to his ears, and Liam smiled.

"I feel better," Liam said, and Troy continued walking closer before stopping right in front of him.

"Is this okay?" Troy asked. Liam nodded, and Troy kissed him. Liam's hands were messy from the cat's breakfast, so he held them away from Troy even as he moved closer. Their bodies touched along with their lips for the first time, and Liam tingled all over. They both jumped back when Manny let out a roar that split the morning. Troy fell to the ground, and Liam stared at him before beginning to laugh.

"Sorry," Liam said, "Manny's just being protective." Liam continued chuckling as he helped Troy to his feet. "He likes to startle people." Liam looked at Manny, and he could have sworn the lion had a self-satisfied look on his face. Then the big cat went back to eating. "I just need to water them and I'm done here. I have other chores to do too." Liam felt bad that he couldn't spend time with Troy, but there was work that he'd let slide for the last few days, and he wanted to get caught up.

"That's okay. Haven asked me to come down today because of this council meeting stuff. He's still trying to figure out what's going on. He's getting a little obsessive."

"He just wants to protect the ranch, since everything around here depends on water. There's a limited amount, and everyone wants some. The ranch has rights because the river runs across the land. You have rights because of the stream on your property."

"But what about the people who've leased the land?" Troy asked as they walked back toward the house.

"If they don't have water on the land, then they don't have any rights, which is probably why they're trying to get the town to agree." Liam stepped inside, and Troy came in as well. Haven was sitting at the table, with maps and papers covering the surface. "I was just explaining the basics of water rights to Troy," Liam explained to Haven.

"What I don't understand is why you really care if the town leases someone their water rights," Troy said before sitting at the table, and Liam thought Haven was going to throttle Troy right there. "Sorry," Troy added. "I really don't understand."

Haven pulled over a map and spread it in front of them. "The river passes through the town before it gets to us. Everyone around here is very careful about what is taken and what's put into the river. The town takes water from the river and purifies it for drinking water and such. But if they let the mining company use their rights, then there's less water for everyone downstream. Part of the year it might be okay, but in the summer, we get enough water, while downstream there's barely enough for the other ranchers. And if the miners take more water, some of the ranches will go dry and then they'll die off. And that's just the water issue. That doesn't take into account the pollution and everything else that comes with the mining operation. There are places where mining has polluted the land to the point where no one can live there."

"There are regulations, you know," Troy said.

"Of course there are, and during the day they follow them. But at night, they're dumping their pollution into the same river we get our water from. Our lives depend upon the land and water. Without either, we're done for. I know I'm probably jumping to conclusions, but I'd rather be safe than sorry." Haven returned to his papers, and Liam watched as he and Troy talked.

"I understand how you feel, I really do," Troy said. "But I don't understand how you can do anything until you know exactly what they want. I know you feel you need to be prepared, but you're jumping to conclusions that could hurt you later."

"Then what do you propose?" Haven asked testily.

"How about we all get back to work," Wally said. "Phillip is here and he's hard at work, so I think we all need to do the same, or there won't be a ranch worth worrying about."

Liam decided to take Wally's advice as an order and hightailed it out of the kitchen. Normally, he'd help in the barn, but if he were truthful, his leg was aching a little, and hauling soiled stall bedding wasn't going to help. "Liam, are you looking for something to do?" Mario asked as he strode across the yard.

"I was thinking of getting a head start on cleaning the cats' enclosures, but they didn't look bad this morning. What do you need?"

"We're going to be moving some of the herd to fresh range. Do you think you can ride a horse?" Mario asked, and Liam smiled before remembering exactly where he was bruised, and he had to shake his head.

"I wish I could, but a saddle or seat is going to rub bad."

"That's cool," Mario replied quickly. "I wasn't sure you were up to it. If I take David with me, do you think you could feed and water the horses?"

"That I can do," Liam replied, relieved that he was able to help. "Is there anything else I can take care of while you're gone? I may as well take care of the dogs too."

Mario patted him on the back. "Thanks. You've been a big help around here." Liam soaked in the praise as Mario walked back toward the barn, and Liam followed, getting started on the chores as the other men saddled horses and then headed out for the rest of the day. Liam took his time making sure all the horses had water, both those left inside and out. He even took the opportunity to clean up some of the water troughs and refill them with fresh water. Then he made sure all the mangers were full. Once he was done, his leg ached, so Liam sat down on a bale of hay in the barn to rest a few minutes before checking everything over one more time.

Then he headed out back to check on the cats, dragging the long hose from the house as he went.

"Let me help with that," Troy said, taking the hose from him. "Wally should think about running water back here directly. That would save all this work every day." Liam nodded and let Troy take the hose, and he returned to the house, turning on the water before walking to the enclosures. It was a hot day, the sun full and bright. Liam washed out each enclosure, dousing each cat in the process, and even Shahrazad seemed grateful. Once he was done, Troy hurried back to turn off the water, and Liam opened the doors to Manny's area. The big cat loped into his area, and Liam closed the doors before opening the ones for Shahrazad, who immediately leapt into the exercise area.

"How do you ever get her to go back into the pen?"

"Meat. She'll only vacate the area if there's food. She's a mean one. Wally told me he's close to a deal to move her to a zoo for a breeding program. It won't be too soon for me." Liam glared at the cat, who yowled sharply back at him. "I think I'm done here for now." Liam went back to the hose and finished rolling it up on his way back to the house. "I'm curious about something," Liam said after placing the coiled hose near the spigot. "When you were married, were you happy?"

"Some of the time," Troy answered.

"Do you want to get married again?" Liam asked.

"No," Troy sighed. "I've thought about things a lot since I've been here, and I've been talking more with my brother, and he's been really understanding and helpful. As kids, we fought a lot, and I see that was probably my fault, because I'm finding out that Kevin is a really great person."

"Were you ashamed of who you are?" Liam asked and then swallowed. "Of being gay, I mean?"

Troy squirmed and shifted from foot to foot, obviously not comfortable with Liam's questions, but these were things he had to know.

Liam had lain awake all night thinking about Troy and what he'd revealed about his past, and he knew it had taken courage to tell him all those things.

"I guess shame is as good a term as any to describe how I felt," Troy admitted, and Liam studied his face, looking for a clue as to how he felt now, but he couldn't see anything.

"Is that what you feel now?" Liam asked cautiously, half afraid of the answer. He'd had to overcome his own shame and self-hatred, so he could understand how Troy had felt, but that wasn't where he was now, and Liam had found that he liked being able to be who he was without apologizing for it to anyone. He'd felt his spirit blossom in the short time he'd been at the ranch, and he was determined to never feel the way he had before ever again.

"I don't know. I feel amazing when I'm with you. Sometimes I wish I knew how I'm supposed to feel."

"I think you're supposed to feel happy and content, and I think you're supposed to be able to tell people you're gay if they ask." Liam saw Troy cringe slightly, and he knew that idea was a little hard for him to get his head around. "I know firsthand how hard it is. It's what I had to do to make the shame and that stomach-clenching feeling whenever someone looked at me like they might know to finally go away most of the time."

Troy swallowed but didn't say anything right away. "Do you have more chores to do?"

"Not until after dinner," Liam answered, and Troy smiled.

"I have my fishing stuff in the truck, and I was wondering if you'd like to go with me?" Troy asked tentatively.

"I have to check with Wally. I'll see you by your truck in a few minutes." Liam hurried inside and found Wally in the office with Phillip, going over the accounts. When he asked for a few hours away, Wally smiled and told him to have a good time, and Liam promised to be back in time for evening chores. He met Troy near the truck and climbed inside, anxious for some time alone with Troy, but a little nervous as well. He pulled on his seatbelt and watched Troy as he started the truck. The ride wasn't long, but Liam found he couldn't stop staring at Troy, and the smile on his face seemed to want to make itself permanent.

When Troy stopped the truck at the base of the track up to Troy's cabin, they both got out. Troy grabbed a tackle box and some fishing poles out of the back, and what looked like an old packing box from behind the seats. "Could you carry this?" Troy asked, and he handed Liam the tackle box. "The trail runs along the creek and it's a little overgrown, so be careful. The fishing spot isn't very far."

Liam took the tackle box and followed Troy into the shade of the small trees that lined the creek. Thankfully, there wasn't much brush and they could walk fairly easily. Troy led him to a clearing near the water where a large tree trunk had bridged the stream. "This is my favorite spot," Troy said, setting down the poles and the box he'd been carrying. "I packed a lunch," Troy told him proudly. "The box doesn't look like much, but it was all I had." Troy set it down and began getting the poles ready. He scooted out onto the log, setting the box next to him on a flattened spot, and Liam did the same, handing Troy the poles. The current was swift, so there was no need to cast their lines. All they needed to do was set their hooks, and the current did the rest. Troy handed him a sandwich, and Liam unwrapped it with one hand and began eating, watching the water as it rushed beneath their perch.

Once he was done, Liam handed Troy the wrapper and Troy gave him a bottle of cold water. "This is nice, peaceful and quiet."

Troy nodded and finished his sandwich before leaning close to him. They shared a light kiss, and Liam felt his heart jump at the tenderness. He'd known very little of that in his life, and it seemed nice to receive it from Troy. The sun shone between the branches, sparkling where it hit the water. Troy handed Liam his pole before pulling off his shirt, shifting on the log until he was sitting on it, and Liam handed him back his pole.

Liam couldn't take his gaze off Troy. Sure, he was older, but you wouldn't really know it. His skin seemed golden as it glistened with a slight sheen of sweat whenever the breeze moved the leaves and the sun sparkled on him. Liam knew he was being silly, but Troy was beautiful, with small nipples that had hardened slightly in the afternoon air and soft lines, barely visible on his stomach. Troy must have seen him looking, because he smiled at him, leaning close and tilting his head slightly. Liam met him halfway, wishing his hands weren't full so he could explore just what Troy's smooth skin felt like. They kissed, and Liam moaned softly, the sound vibrating in his throat, and Troy pressed harder, deepening the kiss. Liam shifted on the log, trying desperately to get his legs into a more comfortable position as his pants tightened. Their kiss gentled, and then Troy pulled his lips away. Their gazes locked, and Liam's breath hitched at the emotion he saw in Troy's. No one had ever looked at him like that, and sometimes in the night, he'd dreamed of seeing that look just once in his life, from anyone. He used to dream he'd see it from his father, the look that said he was most important thing to him, but Liam never had. Instead, he saw the look from Troy, at least he thought he did, because after he blinked it was gone. Liam looked away, averting his eyes to the water, feeling like a child who'd seen something just because he wished it were true.

"What's your family like?" Troy asked him after they'd both been quiet for a while.

"My mom left when I was ten. I can barely remember what she looked like now. I have an old picture of her, but that's all."

"Do you know why she left?" Troy asked, barely above a whisper.

"My dad said it was because of me," Liam replied forcefully. "And I used to believe it." Liam turned toward Troy, old hurt and anger surfacing. "Can you imagine a father telling an eleven-year-old kid that his mother left because of him?" Troy looked shocked at Liam's revelation. "Well, that's what he did. I felt guilty for years and did everything I could to make my father proud of me and make him love me so he wouldn't leave too. Then I figured out that my mother probably left because she got tired of my"—Liam lifted his face to the sky—"asshole father!" Liam shivered with rage, and when he felt Troy's hand on his arm, he jerked away instinctively before the rage flowed away like the water beneath him.

Liam's shirt was stuck to his skin. He shifted to get comfortable before handing Troy his pole and pulling off his shirt. The air felt good on his skin, so he draped the sweaty garment over the log before retrieving his pole from Troy. Liam felt Troy's gaze. He tried not to shy away, and when Troy leaned close again, he tried not to jump when he felt Troy's lips on his shoulder. Reeling in his line, Liam checked it before releasing it and letting the current take it again. Liam turned at the sound of cattle close by. At first he thought some had gotten out and into the woods, but there was no other sound. When he heard it again, he realized the sound was simply carrying. The gasp he heard from behind him startled him, and he tipped backward, nearly toppling until he felt Troy's hand help balance him.

"What happened to you?" Troy's light touch on his back made him shiver as he touched sensitive skin.

"Another gift from the asshole," Liam said, his anger returning. "My father believed in not sparing the rod and spoiling the child. Once my mother left, he took his rage out on me for the slightest infraction." Liam turned so Troy couldn't see the marks on his back, scars that the doctors had told him he'd have for the rest of his life. "I tried to please him, and that only made things worse for me, because I ended up with disappointment on top of the pain. After a while I stopped feeling either one."

"Is that why you left? Not that I'd blame you."

"No. I left because he found out I was gay, and I figured if he got his hands on me, I'd end up dead. I got a job at a ranch a ways from home, but it only lasted one day. I didn't think of it at the time, but they fired me so quickly, I think now it was because my dad found out where I was and called them." Anger simmered below the surface, and he began to squirm on the log. If he were someplace else, he'd be walking or cleaning stalls, anything to give himself something to do. Instead, he sat and felt like he was going to crawl out of his skin. "After that I made my way north, and

Wally found me and brought me here." He didn't relate the details; they really weren't important.

"Wally said you'd had it tough. Does he know what you've told me?"

Liam looked to Troy. "Most of it."

"There's more, isn't there?" Troy said softly, and Liam stared back down at the water, letting his head hang, wishing he could be someone else and forget. "What happened?"

"After I was kicked off the ranch, they at least had the decency to pay me for the work I'd done. I couldn't get a job anywhere, so I began hitching, and I did things to get rides." Liam's voice faltered. "Things I wouldn't have done if I wasn't so tired and hungry that I didn't know if I could last another day. By the time I got here, I couldn't take another step. My water was gone, and I fell into a ditch and prayed to die. I barely had enough energy to breathe. That's when Wally found me. He helped me, and then he and Haven gave me a job and a home." Liam swallowed hard, still having trouble believing his good fortune after nearly a lifetime of abuse and misery. "He saved me."

Troy was quiet for a while, and Liam stared into the water. "I think that's what Wally does." Troy's comment hit home, and Liam nodded slowly. The sound of his line playing out brought Liam out of his thoughts, and he grabbed the rod and began reeling in the line, suddenly very excited, his pain slipping from his mind.

"Easy, reel the fish in easy," Troy coached.

Liam shifted on the log and continued reeling, his heart pounding with excitement as the trout came into sight. "I can't believe I caught one!" he cried, forgetting about everything except getting the fish. Troy stepped over him and returned with a net. As soon as the fish broke the water, Troy scooped it up and brought it so Liam could lift it out of the net. "It's a beaut!" Troy said, and Liam had to agree.

"A trout!"

"It certainly is. Let's get this baby into the bucket." Troy brought a large container, and Liam removed the hook and dropped the fish into the container. After watching it flip and flop for a few seconds, Troy put a towel over the top and set the container away from the water, and they returned to their seats on the log. Liam rebaited his hook and put the line in the water again. Troy passed him another sandwich, and Liam ate it with a smile on his face. "So what did you do before you came here?" Liam asked, thankful that he could shift the conversation to Troy.

"I worked for the Department of the Interior in Washington. I was your regular garden-variety bureaucrat."

"Are they the ones who leased the land to the mining company?" Liam asked.

"Probably. I worked in the section that handled the budgets for the national parks. I'm not really up on how land leases for mining work." Troy seemed a little nervous. "If I could help, I would."

Liam nodded. He believed Troy, and smiled as the other man leaned in to kiss him. The same sound of line playing out interrupted them again, though this time it was Troy's, and they both laughed as Liam got the net and Troy reeled in his fish. "Maybe it's the kisses," Liam said as he scooped up the fish.

"Could be," Troy answered, and after placing Troy's fish with his, Liam settled back on the log, and they spent the rest of the afternoon talking. Having already told Troy about the hard stuff, Liam relaxed and told Troy all kinds of stories, and Troy did the same. By the time they'd reeled in a total of five fish, they were both happy, and they'd truly confirmed that kisses seemed to be the magic ingredient.

Having caught enough fish, they slid off the log and started packing up. Liam began putting his shirt back on, and he felt Troy skim his hands lightly over his chest. "You really are incredible," Troy said, and when Liam lowered the shirt, Troy kissed him. The other kisses had been gentle and soft, but this one was hard and deep, sending a wave of passion through Liam so intense he thought his knees would buckle.

Liam steadied his legs, willing them not to bend as Troy's arms tugged him closer. He could barely think of anything other than the feel of Troy's lips on his and the warmth that radiated through his thin shirt. Returning Troy's embrace, Liam felt the smooth skin of Troy's back, stroking it with his hands. Nearly all his life, he'd dreamed of being held like this by someone who cared about him. The kiss gentled, and Liam felt Troy pull his lips away, and stroke a hand along his cheek. Liam soaked in the attention like a dry sponge, afraid to open his eyes or he'd realize this was a dream. "Are you ashamed of me? Of us?" Liam asked softly.

"No," Troy answered, his voice soft and husky. "I'm coming to realize that the way I felt about myself was keeping me from being happy. You make me happy, Liam."

Liam couldn't ignore the undertone of pain in Troy's voice, and he opened his eyes, half expecting to wake up. Before he could figure out the cause, Troy was hugging him tightly, pressing their bodies together. Liam's reacted forcefully until he realized this wasn't romantic. Troy was clinging to him with everything he had. "I'm sorry," Troy said in Liam's ear and began to pull away, but Liam held him tight.

"It's okay," Liam soothed.

"No, it's not. I've messed up everything in my life. What if I mess this up too?" Fear filled Troy's eyes. Liam didn't know what to say, so he stayed quiet and let Troy get out what he needed to. "I really could."

"That's the shame talking, and you've got to let it go," Liam said quietly, not sure at all what to say, because anything he tried to say would just be words until Troy allowed himself to move past what he felt in his heart. Liam knew a lifetime of hurt didn't go away overnight, so he figured a lifetime of shame and denial wouldn't either. Troy's bear-hug loosened, and his head lifted off Liam's shoulders, their eyes meeting.

"What if I can't, and what if I hurt you because of it?"

"I'm strong," Liam answered. The words triggered something in his mind, and he realized he truly was. He'd lived through and survived a great deal of pain. Granted, he wanted to be happy and leave that behind him. "And if I'm willing to take the chance on you, then maybe you should too." Liam smiled slightly before capturing Troy's lips in a kiss of his own, deepening it, taking charge of it, and Troy let him. Up to now that was all they'd done, but Liam wanted more and he took it, sliding his hands down Troy's back. Liam's cock throbbed painfully in his pants, and he felt Troy's against his hip. Recently, Liam's sexual encounters had been out of his control, and right now with Troy, Liam felt powerful as he listened to Troy's small whimpers.

Troy stroked beneath Liam's shirt, and Liam continued kissing him, his hands roaming freely now across Troy's skin, stroking his chest, fingering the small, pert nipples, and even daring to feel down Troy's stomach. Liam felt Troy's breath hitch, and he broke the kiss, looking into Troy's eyes. They were clouded with passion, half-lidded, and he heard Troy's soft panting. Feeling emboldened, Liam opened the snap at Troy's waist, and the fabric of his jeans seemed to part on its own. Sliding his hand down Troy's skin once again, Liam didn't stop this time, slipping his fingers beneath the elastic waistband before skimming over Troy's length.

"Liam, please don't tease."

After what he'd done on the road, Liam hadn't been sure how he'd feel when it came time to be intimate with someone, but those thoughts were the furthest thing from his mind as he concentrated on Troy and the way his own heart pounded in his chest at each and every touch. He moved his fingers to encircle Troy's length, and he watched as Troy's eyes widened and he went completely still. "Is this okay?" Liam asked, and Troy nodded.

"I can't believe how your hand feels," Troy gasped, and Liam tightened his grip. "Jesus!" Troy cried, and Liam felt Troy start to move his hips. Then he felt his own pants part. Liam gasped when Troy freed his erection from the confines of the fabric. The air felt good on his skin, but Troy's fingers felt even better. Liam held Troy, and Troy held him, as though they each needed the other to keep from falling over. Liam knew he wasn't going to last long, and bit his lip slightly to try to stem the tide of his almost instantly overwhelming climax. Troy's hips moved, and

Liam went with it, moving his own. Troy's cock slid through Liam's fingers as Liam's own slid through Troy's, the combined sensations quickly adding to his excitement, and through his haze of passion Liam felt Troy's entire body begin to shake. "Liam, can't...."

"Don't try... just go... with it," Liam gasped, and he felt Troy throb in his hands as he did the same, with Liam right behind him trying his best to stay upright through the waves of pleasure that hit his entire quivering body. Liam clamped his eyes closed and let his body have its way until he could no longer keep his balance, and he leaned against Troy, who seemed to have the same issue, and together they tumbled into a heap on the soft earth.

After catching his breath, Liam opened his eyes and saw Troy do the same. Liam smiled, and Troy followed along, and then they both began to chuckle as they realized their bare asses sat on the dirt and neither of them gave a damn. It took them a while to get back to their feet and put themselves to rights, but they both grinned like cats as they dressed. The smiles faded as Troy pulled him into a hug and kissed him hard, with a deep passion that told Liam that there was no regret and shame in what they'd done.

"We should get you back to the ranch for afternoon chores," Troy said, and they began gathering their things and carrying them to the truck. "How's your leg?" Troy asked once they had everything loaded.

"A little sore," Liam lied. His leg throbbed, but he didn't want Troy to feel bad. Liam had had a wonderful time, and he didn't want anything to spoil it. Once he got back to the ranch, he'd finish his afternoon chores and rest for a while. Climbing into the truck, Liam stretched out his leg, and they both rode home with smiles on their faces. Those grins lasted until Troy pulled into the drive, and Liam saw a familiar truck parked off to the side. "What's he doing here?" Liam asked as a shot of fear raced through his body.

"Who?" Troy asked.

"My father," Liam said as levelly as he could, just as his father stepped out of the barn and looked through the truck windows. Their eyes met, and the same insecurity he'd felt since he was a child surged through him. The truck pulled to a stop, and Liam barely registered Troy making a phone call. For Liam, the entire world seemed to narrow to just him and his father, and that world was filled with fear, intimidation, and insecurity. It almost felt as if he'd been transported back to when he was ten years old. Liam had thought he'd gotten far enough away that his father wouldn't be able to find him, but that obviously hadn't been the case.

Chapter Six

TROY hung up the phone after making a fast call to Wally. He didn't know what else to do, but after the stories Liam had told him and then seeing the man show up without any warning, combined with what Troy could only describe as an evil look in the man's eyes, Troy figured Liam's father was going to be trouble—and Liam had already known enough of that. Troy looked at Liam, watching as he stared at his father without moving.

"Wally's on his way," Troy said. "Just stay where you are, and if he does anything, we can be out of here fast."

"No, it's fine," Liam said softly, and he began to open his door. Troy wasn't sure that was such a good idea, but the man was Liam's father, and his own son perhaps knew him best. Troy got out, closing his door with a slam, and followed Liam as he walked toward the barn. "What are you doing here, Dad?" Troy noticed the way Liam seemed to spit out the word "Dad," like he was cursing.

"You're my son, and I was worried about you," the man answered in an understanding tone that shocked Troy.

"You haven't worried about me since I was ten, so why start now? Besides, it's a long way to come just for that. What do you want?" Liam asked firmly, but Troy could see the way his leg shook slightly in his jeans.

"You to stop this silliness and come back home to work the ranch," Liam's father ground out between his teeth. Now, *there* was the tone Troy had expected, demanding and entitled. Liam turned to look at Troy, who stepped a little closer. "That's another thing, now that you've seen how hard it is to be on your own, I suspect you're ready to give up this ridiculous gay notion and settle down like any God-fearing, normal man."

The sound of truck tires on the drive made everyone look, and Wally cruised to a stop and got out, striding over to join them. "You have five minutes to get yourself off this ranch." Wally had himself worked up to a good head of steam.

Liam's father huffed and stepped closer, but Liam intervened. "It's okay, Wally. He was just leaving, and he isn't coming back. I'm not his whipping boy any longer, and I have no intention of returning to the ranch and working like some slave." Liam turned back to his dad. "I don't need you anymore, and you aren't welcome here." Liam sounded so confident, but Troy knew what he was witnessing was pure guts with just a bit of bravado.

"Now listen here." Liam's father reached for his arm, and Liam stepped back just out of reach.

"No, you listen. I know you came here for more than just to see me or to offer me a place at the ranch. You're too selfish and manipulative to come this far for something like that. I know you want something from me, and you aren't going to get it." Liam stood his ground, and Troy stepped forward, standing right behind Liam when his father tried to intimidate him. "What is it you really want?"

A myriad of expressions quickly passed over Liam's father's face. Troy had never met the man before, but he'd dealt with plenty of people like him over the years. Hell, Troy was just like him, or had been. Whenever he hadn't gotten what he wanted, he'd bullied his brother, and even his parents, until they'd given in. Troy stared at Liam's father and then looked at Liam, who seemed as determined as he'd ever seen him.

"I have an offer on the ranch, and the lawyer says I need your signature."

"Then you can send me the papers, and I'll look them over. That's the best I'm willing to give you, and more than you deserve," Liam said.

Wally stepped forward, the smaller man staring down Liam's much larger father. "Now I suggest you go."

"And what if I don't want to, little big man?" Liam's father stepped toward Wally, and before Troy knew what had happened, the bigger man was planted ass-first in the dirt, rubbing his jaw.

"I told you to leave. Next time you'll be carried off my land." Wally scowled. "You don't threaten me or any of the people on this ranch, and that includes your son." Wally continued staring at Liam's father as he picked himself up off the ground, giving Wally a wide berth as he made his way to his truck.

"You know Liam's a fag, don't you? Are you sure you want his type here?" Liam's father growled.

"His type? You mean *my type,* because you just got your ass kicked by a fag—one half your size—and I'll do it again in a heartbeat. So I'll say this just one more time: get your ugly, fat ass off my ranch." Wally took a step toward the truck, and Liam's father got inside, holding an envelope out the window that Liam snatched out of his hand as his father gunned the truck, sending up a cloud of dust as he drove down the drive and out to the street.

Liam seemed to deflate as soon as his father was out of sight. "Thanks, Wally."

"No thanks necessary. If only half the things you've told me are true, I'd have enjoyed kicking his ass from here to kingdom come." Wally dusted himself off and turned his gaze from the receding truck to where they were standing. "And as for you, mister, don't think I didn't see you limping because your leg is hurting. Go on inside and rest on the sofa." Mama Wally was out in full force, and Troy had to keep himself from snickering, until Wally turned to him. "You should be paying better attention," Wally scolded, but when Troy got the container of fish, Wally's mood brightened considerably.

"I thought you could have fish for dinner," Troy said as a peace offering.

"You caught them, you clean them," Wally said as he walked toward the house. "Save the scraps and we'll feed them to the cats. They'll love them," Wally added with half a smile before shooing Liam into the house.

Troy cleaned the fish, leaving the innards and stuff in the bucket, and when he carried the fish inside, Wally excused himself, most likely to go give the cats their treat. When he returned, Wally began preparing the fish for dinner, while Troy joined Liam and Jefferson in the living room, where Liam was looking over the papers. "I don't understand any of this."

"We'll find a lawyer and have him look it over," Troy suggested, and Liam set the papers aside. The house seemed unusually quiet. "Where are Haven and Phillip?" Troy asked.

"I told Haven he needed to move his anti-mining campaign to his own house, not that there's much he can do until the council meeting in a few days." Troy thought he heard a touch of worry in Wally's voice. Not that he blamed him—this could change the way of life on the ranch and threaten its existence if what Haven said was right, and Troy had no reason to doubt him.

"What are you going to do?" Troy asked, expecting Wally to answer.

"Fight," Jefferson answered from his wheelchair. "We will fight with everything we have."

Troy didn't know what to say about that. His own land wasn't under threat, but Liam's new home was, and that was enough to get Troy's dander up. "Don't worry," Jefferson continued, "we know how to do that. We've fought before and we'll do it again." Jefferson got quiet for a while, and Troy could almost feel the man's gaze on him.

"Can I get you something?" Troy asked Jefferson, but he appeared to ignore the question and closed his eyes. Troy turned his attention to Liam, who had his eyes closed as well. "Do you need anything?" Troy asked softly.

"No," Liam answered, taking Troy's hand and holding it before closing his eyes again. "When was the last time you saw your daughter?" Liam asked. "I guess my dad's 'visit' made me think of your family."

"Four months ago, I suppose." Troy swallowed at the memory.

"You should see her," Liam said softly, sounding half asleep. "She deserves to know her daddy." Liam said no more, and Troy hoped he was asleep.

"He's right," Jefferson added from his chair. "I don't know what you think you've done, but there ain't nothing so bad as to keep you away from your child." Troy opened his mouth to explain, but closed it again. There was no way that anyone could possibly understand. "We don't know your situation, but that little girl deserves to know that you love her, and you staying away is only hurting her."

"She said she hated me," Troy said softly.

"The line between hate and love is only a hair wide," Jefferson observed. "She deserves to know you, and then she can make up her mind on her own about what she wants. She can't be very old because you aren't much more than a baby yourself. So you still have time," Jefferson said before resting his head back against the rest and closing his eyes one more time.

With both of them asleep, Troy quietly walked into the kitchen. "I should head home," he told Wally.

"You'll do no such thing. You and Liam provided dinner, so you can stay to eat it." Wally went back to dipping the fish in flour, getting it ready to sauté. "Liam will be disappointed if you're not here."

"You really are like a mother hen, aren't you?" Troy joked.

Wally stopped what he was doing and turned toward Troy. "When it comes to him, yes. He hasn't had it easy a day in his life, and yet he's outgoing and smiles at everyone with hardly a cross word. Don't forget he risked himself because he thought you were hurt. He'd do that for anyone on this ranch; I know that. I may not have known him long, but I already know that he has a special heart, and if you break it, you'll have to answer to me. But if you nurture it, that young man could be the greatest gift you've ever received in your life." Wally turned back to his cooking. "Sorry for getting preachy. You'd think it was Sunday."

Troy peered around the corner, watching Liam's quiet form as he slept on the sofa, his leg propped up. "I never set out to hurt anyone," Troy said softly, almost to himself.

"Most people don't," Wally said as he continued working at the stove. He finished flouring the fish and set them aside, opening the refrigerator door and pulling out the makings for salad. "Jefferson's a smart man," Wally commented after closing the refrigerator door. Troy didn't turn to look. He knew what Jefferson had said was probably true, but he wasn't sure he was ready to face his family. "It probably wouldn't hurt to call."

"Sofia never talks to me," Troy said, trying not to let the hurt creep into his voice. The sound of a chair scraping on the floor caused him to turn around. Troy saw Wally sitting at the table, looking like he was waiting for something. Troy sighed and sat down, quietly telling Wally the same things he'd told Liam. While he hated telling the story, once he was done, Troy had to admit he felt better. Neither Wally nor Liam had judged him.

"If you want my opinion," Wally said once Troy was through, "you need to start with Jeanie. The two of you need to make peace with each other. You say you loved her, and she probably needs to hear that, and that your entire marriage wasn't a lie."

"I did tell her that," Troy countered.

"Yes. But she wasn't ready or able to hear it through the hurt." Wally got up and went back to the counter, starting to make the salad. "Think about it." He began cutting a tomato, and Troy expected him to say more, but he didn't. After a while, Troy went back into the living room and quietly sat with the two sleeping men, watching Liam. He looked so sweet, almost angelic, when he slept.

"How long have you been sitting there?" Liam asked, his blue eyes fluttering open.

"Not too long," Troy answered, moving to sit near the edge of the sofa. "How's your leg?"

"Better. The pain's going away. I think I just needed to rest it." Liam moved to sit up, but Troy put his hand lightly on his shoulder, so Liam reclined once again.

"Take it easy," Troy soothed.

Liam nodded. "I keep thinking about my dad. If he's come all this way, I don't think he's going to leave town just like that. He's going to cause trouble."

"We can handle whatever he tries to pull," Jefferson said, his voice slurred but understandable. "Don't you worry about that, young man."

Troy silently agreed with him. If anyone could protect Liam from anything, it was Wally.

Liam's mouth broke into a smile, and Troy cocked his head in curiosity. "I'm just remembering the look on my dad's face when Wally laid him out. I half expected to see him scratch his butt, trying to figure out what the hell had happened." Liam began to laugh. "Did you see the look on his face when Wally told him he was gay? I thought he was going to shit bricks sitting on his butt in the dirt." Liam laughed, and Troy chuckled along. For him, it wasn't particularly funny, but Troy figured that for Liam to see his abusive father put in his place would be cause for celebration.

"I wouldn't have thought Wally could do that," Troy commented, and he realized he'd made assumptions because of Wally's size—the exact same mistake Liam's father had.

"It's not the first time," Wally said, his voice drifting in from the kitchen. "And I'm sad to say it probably won't be the last." Troy heard the fish sear as Wally placed them in the pan. The front door opened, and Troy saw Dakota walk quietly into the house. Troy was about to say hello when he saw Dakota put his finger over his lips and tilt his head toward the kitchen. Dakota walked quietly through the house, and Troy heard Wally squeak, followed by a whoop, and then silence. Troy didn't need much of an imagination to know what the silence meant.

After a while, Dakota returned to the living room and greeted his father, as well, before shaking hands with each of them. Troy fidgeted under Dakota's strange look when Liam took his hand. "I take it you two have settled your differences." Liam grinned and nodded as Troy did the same.

"What are you home for, son?" Jefferson asked.

"I got someone to take my shifts for a few days. I wanted to be here for this council meeting," Dakota told his father before sitting down. Dakota had just taken his seat when Wally called them all for dinner.

Dakota wheeled his father to the table and then sat next to Wally, while Troy sat next to Liam. "Where did you get the fish?" Dakota asked. "They look amazing."

"Liam and Troy caught them," Wally answered. "I put the other two in the freezer for you," he told Troy before passing the platter around the table. The fish weren't large trout, but they were certainly tasty, and everyone ate their fill. Liam and Wally took turns bringing Dakota up to date on all the happenings around the ranch, and Liam took particular delight in relating the incident with his father.

"I can pass the papers on to my lawyer, if you like," Dakota offered, and Liam promised to give them to him right after dinner.

"They're complete gobbledygook to me," Liam explained, looking relieved. "I know my dad's trying to pull something, I just don't know what."

"We'll get to the bottom of it," Wally said after swallowing. "Don't worry." Word that Dakota was back must have gotten out to the hands, because a steady stream of workers and friends came through the house, with exchanges of many hugs and handshakes. Troy helped Wally clean up the table and then sat next to Liam in the living room, soaking in his body heat and the light musky scent that every now and then would reach his nose and drive him crazy.

"I have to feed and water the cats," Liam said as he stood up from the sofa, and Troy swore he looked at Wally, daring him to say anything.

"I'll help you," Troy offered, and he followed Liam outside. It didn't take long before the cats were munching on their dinner and Troy was following Liam back toward the house. Troy noticed a slight limp, but it didn't seem to slow Liam down. "I should probably head up home," Troy said as they approached the back door.

Liam reached out to him, touching Troy's arm lightly. "Stay."

Troy stopped and looked through the window into the house. He saw Wally working in the kitchen, and Dakota walking up behind him. Troy could not see what was happening, but the smile on Wally's face left no doubt as to how happy he was to have the other man home. Troy looked away when Wally turned around and Dakota leaned in close. That was too personal, but it was one of the most loving sights he'd ever seen.

Liam's eyes shone back at him, and he moved closer. "I want what they have," Liam said softly as he placed his arms around Troy's waist, leaning his head against Troy's shoulder. Troy swallowed the fear welling up inside him. He wished more than anything that he could give that to Liam, but Troy wasn't sure he was capable of it, and Liam seemed to read his mind. "Quit worrying about the past and do something about it. I can't change mine, and you can't change yours. All we can do is live with it and make it right if we can."

"You sound like Wally," Troy observed.

"I'll take that as a compliment," Liam quipped and angled his face up toward Troy's expectantly, and there was no way Troy could turn an offer like that down. He kissed softly, and it was Liam who moved his arms around Troy's neck, deepening the kiss in an instant. Troy was fast learning that Liam knew what he wanted and wasn't as shy as Troy expected about asking for it or even taking it. Not that there was a single thing wrong with a man who knew what he wanted, especially when it involved lips that made him shiver and a tongue that did things to make his head throb. Troy's pants tightened measurably as he returned the kiss, giving as good as he was getting. "Stay with me, Troy."

"Are you sure Wally and Dakota won't mind?" Troy asked as most of the lights went off inside the house.

"I somehow doubt that they'll care about anything apart from each other tonight," Liam answered and began slowly walking them both around to the front door. The yard was quiet and still. Together they sat on the porch bench, arms around each other. Troy kept trying to override the instinct to run and hide. It wasn't until he looked into Liam's eyes once again that the urge left him. After sitting quietly for a while, Liam stood and took Troy's hand, leading him through the nearly silent house to his room and closing the door behind them.

Troy stared into Liam's eyes, feeling as nervous as he could ever remember. Slowly, Liam approached him, and Troy's pulse rate sped up as Liam pressed his hand just above his heart. Closer and closer he moved, as though everything were happening in slow motion. Then Liam was kissing him and holding him close. Troy had had plenty of sex with men— impersonal, no names given sex—not that he was proud of it, but he had. And never before had it felt like this. There was the usual rush and the surge of desire that he'd felt before. But there was also something more, something Troy hadn't felt with anyone, even Jeanie—a connection that he couldn't quite describe. For a split second, Troy tried to name it and put his finger on it. But Liam had other ideas, and that included a tongue that seemed to possess his mouth. Liam's weight pressed closer to him, and Troy backed up until the edge of the mattress touched the back of his legs. Then he tumbled, bouncing slightly, with Liam on top of him, pressing him into the mattress, kissing Troy even harder.

Liam felt like a live wire, all energy and desire, as he writhed on top of Troy in the absolute best way possible. Troy could not remember ever having had this effect on anyone before, and he found it the greatest turn-on in the world. Liam slipped his hands beneath Troy's shirt, and Troy sighed into the kiss as Liam stroked his skin. And when Liam fingered one of Troy's nipples, Troy started at the sensation and gasped when Liam pulled his lips away before lifting Troy's shirt, sucking on one of the firm buds. Troy writhed on the bed, thrusting his chest forward for more, and Liam obliged. Little nips and bites blazed a trail on skin that was rapidly heating up. Troy's hips seemed to have a mind of their own, thrusting into the air as his desire quickly ramped up. Then Liam's face lifted, and they kissed again, hard and deep, with Troy whimpering under the onslaught of Liam's fingers plucking his still sensitized buds.

"Liam!" Troy cried as Liam clamped his lips once again around a nipple, doing this circle thing with his tongue that was driving Troy out of his mind. For a brief second, Troy wondered where Liam had learned to do the things he was doing, but then he felt fingers at his belt, opening it, tugging at the waistband of his jeans until the fabric seemed to part whether it wanted to or not. "You're going to kill me," Troy moaned softly.

Liam chuckled softly. "Not for a very long time if I can help it." Then Liam kissed him again, and Troy gasped into the kiss as Liam tightened his fingers around his length. Troy tried to thrust, but Liam only held him tighter, increasing his need and desire.

Troy groaned when Liam released him before pulling his shirt over his head. Liam stopped when Troy's head popped out of the T-shirt, the fabric still on his arms. "Leave them there," Liam commanded, and Troy's eyebrows shot up, but he was so far gone, desire and passion completely ruling him now, that he did as Liam instructed. Troy's breath was shallow and fast as he felt Liam's weight shift off the bed. Liam pulled off Troy's shoes and then his pants. Troy felt completely wicked and wanton, naked and hard with Liam still dressed, looking at him like he was some sort of buffet.

"I've wanted to see you like this almost from the day we met." Liam graciously left out the gun thing, although Troy's gun felt like it was going to go off at any second. "You're a handsome man, Troy."

"So are you," Troy answered, squirming on the bed, willing silently for Liam to touch him, but the man seemed determined to make Troy wait.

"Just relax and take it easy," Liam said softly. "Anticipation is half the fun."

"Where'd you learn that?" Troy asked, wondering who he had to thank for that little gem.

"I have a vivid imagination, and I always wanted to have a hunky man laid out and naked for me. This is one of the things I always saw when I closed my eyes, someone who was my own, excited and waiting just for me."

Damn if that wasn't the hottest thing Troy had ever heard come out of anyone's mouth, and he groaned when Liam stepped farther away from the bed. He was tempted to shuck away the shirt from his hands—he could do it easily—but he wanted to please Liam, and if that made him happy, it made Troy happy. Hell, it made Troy fucking, throbbing happy, if he admitted the truth.

Troy watched as Liam pulled off his shirt and then toed off his shoes. This was no striptease, hell no. This was a Texas-born man getting nekkid, and Troy was enjoying the view. When Liam's pants dropped and he stepped out of them with everything the good Lord gave him on display, Troy felt his mouth water. "Go ahead and shift up on the bed, but leave your hands in the shirt," Liam said.

"Do you like having me at your mercy?" Troy asked, a little surprised at just how much this was turning him on. *Who knew?*

Liam nodded and waited for Troy to get into position before prowling onto the bed like one of the cats he took care of. "You better believe it." Liam lightly stroked up Troy's thighs and then over his nipples, skimming his fingers along his Troy's length. "I love the sounds you make and the way you shiver under my hands." Liam moved closer, and Troy spread his legs as Liam moved between them, brushing his calves against Troy's as he skimmed his hands over Troy's now hypersensitive nipples and moved his lips so close to Troy's that he could feel the heat from Liam's skin.

"You've really thought about this a lot, haven't you?" Troy asked with a smile before Liam kissed him again.

"Yes. I've had years to fantasize about exactly this." Liam didn't even crack a smile. His gaze seared into Troy, and whatever he was about to say flew out of mind. Liam looked as though Troy was the Holy Grail, and there was no way Troy ever wanted that look to fade. Saying to hell with it, Troy slipped his hands out of the shirt and pulled Liam to him, hugging the man to his body as tightly as he could, wanting as much skin-to-skin contact as possible.

Troy sighed loudly as his cock slid along Liam's hip, and he felt Liam's against his own skin. Troy could not remember the last time he'd been touched like this. Even with Jeanie, this type of intimacy had been missing from their marriage for quite some time. Troy knew why, but that didn't make his need for it any less. Placing his hands on Liam's cheeks, he guided their lips together in a kiss that sent him reeling.

Troy's hips bucked slowly, and he felt Liam doing the same, their kisses intensifying as their bodies moved against one another. Their kisses continued, and Troy ran his hands gently down Liam's back, the scars he knew were there passing under his fingers, and he felt Liam still. "You have nothing to be ashamed of," Troy said to reassure Liam. "They're like trophies of war, and you should wear them proudly. You endured each and every one." Troy didn't give Liam a chance to respond as he kissed him again, letting his hands roam lower before lightly cupping Liam's butt.

Troy used his hand placement as leverage and pressed their bodies together even harder, bucking more forcefully so he could get just that much more friction. Liam pulled his lips away, arching his back as he thrust against Troy. He could hear Liam's breathing become ragged along with his rhythm. Troy could feel his release building, though he wanted to hold off for Liam. More than anything, Troy wanted to see him, watch his face as he climaxed. So through sheer force of will, Troy kept a modicum of control until he heard Liam's small cries and saw him throw his head back, mouth hanging open, and then Troy felt Liam's release. All those sensations pulled away the last of Troy's control, and he followed Liam into his own orgasm that blurred his vision.

"Troy," Liam said softly, and he stroked Troy's back, breathing deeply as they both slowly came down from their passion.

Liam smiled at him, and then they kissed languidly. Slowly, Liam shifted off Troy's body before quietly leaving the room, returning with a cloth that they used to clean themselves up. Then Liam pushed open the window, letting in the fresh air along with the soft sounds of the ranch at night, horses nickering, the low sounds of cattle, and the chirping of a million crickets. Liam climbed back into the bed, and they curled together before Liam reached over him and clicked off the small light near the bed.

The darkness engulfed them, and Troy closed his eyes, listening to the sounds from outside and Liam's soft breathing as he slowly rubbed his hands along Liam's arm. Troy found, to his surprise, that he was content, a feeling he almost couldn't remember, and he was afraid to close his eyes because then morning would come and the world would intrude. Liam stroked Troy's cheek, and he leaned into the touch, encouraging the light caress. He needed it from Liam almost as much as he needed to breathe.

"Go to sleep," Liam whispered, and Troy could almost hear the smile in his voice.

"I can't," Troy answered before kissing Liam lightly on the cheek. "I don't want to miss a minute with you." Troy didn't get an answer to that, but he felt Liam snuggle up, and Liam's arm around his chest held him just a little closer. Eventually, Troy fell into a light sleep.

It was a change in the sounds from outside that woke him. At first Troy thought it was the sound of morning on the ranch, but pounding hooves did not seem right, and he nudged Liam awake. "Is something wrong outside?" Troy asked, and he felt Liam sit up and still for a second before jumping out of bed. Troy turned on the light in time to see Liam's butt disappearing into his jeans. "What is it?"

"The horses are loose!" Liam said with a touch of fear in his voice, shrugging on his shirt and jamming his feet into his shoes as Troy began getting dressed as well. The bedroom door opened, and Wally hurried in, saw them already dressing, and closed the door again. Troy heard additional footsteps in the hall, and then Liam was out the door. Troy threw the last of his clothes on in a hurry before rushing through the quiet house and out into the bustling yard.

"What happened?" Troy asked the first person he came across.

"Every door was opened, stalls, paddocks, you name it. Even the gates to the ranges were opened, but it looks like the cattle hadn't found them yet," Mario answered, dressed in only a pair of jeans and shoes as he hurried across the yard. "Can you help in the barn? We've got people rounding up the horses and we'll need to get them settled."

Troy nodded and hurried to the barn as Dakota walked a horse across the yard. "Which stall?" Troy asked.

"Second on the right," Dakota answered, and Troy went inside, pulling the door Dakota indicated fully open and closing it after the horse. "Thanks," Dakota said hastily before hurrying back outside. Other people came in leading horses, and Troy held the stall doors.

"Treats are there," Liam explained when he came in, pointing to a bag near the feed. "Give them each one; it will help calm them down."

"I will," Troy answered, and Liam hurried off again. The flow of horses trickled off quickly, but many of the stalls were still unoccupied. After waiting half an hour, he heard hooves outside the door, and Wally walked inside. "Where is everyone?"

Wally led the huge horse into the stall, Troy closing the door. "We're finding them way down the way. This one was near the east range, beside the main road. We'll be lucky if one of them isn't hit by a passing car," Wally explained angrily. Troy knew he wasn't the source of the anger and let it go as Wally stormed out of the barn. Mario came in, along with Liam, each of them leading a horse.

"There are still four missing," Mario explained with worry in his voice. "We'd better get an ATV, because they could be anywhere by now." Troy closed the stall doors and gave each horse a treat, talking low to them the way he'd seen Liam soothe the large beasts. Dakota came in a few minutes later, leading another horse, which they put in a stall.

"Come on, I could use your help," Dakota instructed, both his voice and body tight with tension. "We'll take an ATV and see if we can locate the missing horses. We'll need to ride double so I can lead the horse back if we find one." Dakota strode toward the equipment shed, and Troy hurried to keep up. Both of them jumped onto a single ATV. "Hang on," Dakota yelled, and Troy complied before the man took off like a bat out of hell.

Troy held on for all he was worth as they bounced over the road. Dawn was just beginning to show in the east when Troy spotted what looked like a horse near the edge of the road. He tapped Dakota on the shoulder and pointed. Thankfully, Dakota slowed down, stopping a ways from the horse. Dakota turned off the engine and slowly approached the animal, which looked about ready to bolt, but Dakota got the horse by the halter and motioned for Troy to head back to the barn.

Troy turned the ATV around and headed back, parking the vehicle back in the shed once he saw that others had congregated. "Dakota's leading back a horse," Troy told Wally, who looked immensely relieved.

"That seems like the last of them," Wally said before turning to the men. "I hate to ask, but we'd better check the fences in case the bastard who did this didn't stop at just opening gates." Troy looked over at Liam, seeing him fidgeting, and he knew Liam was thinking the exact same thing he was: this was too much of a coincidence.

"I'm going to feed the cats," Liam told Wally, who nodded, and Troy followed him around the house, once again noticing Liam's limp. Troy assisted with the feeding as best he could by helping Liam prepare the food, but he let Liam handle the actual feeding. Once he was done and the cats had been switched out of the exercise area, they walked back toward the house.

"I should go up home and check on things. I know you have chores to do," Troy said outside the back door. "And I can tell your leg's hurting."

"It is, but not too bad. The jostling has it thumping, and Wally already made me promise to get off it for a while this morning," Liam said. Troy leaned in close, giving him a gentle kiss before watching Liam go inside, and then he walked around to his truck, got in, and drove up to the cabin.

He parked and got out, walking into the cabin. Everything seemed the same as it had when he'd left, and yet it wasn't. Making himself something to eat, Troy sat at his small table alone and half expected to hear Wally talking about one of his patients, or Haven grumbling about the upcoming council meeting as he wondered out loud about what would happen. The place was just quiet. When Troy had first come here, this was what he'd thought he wanted. But he missed the conversations, and he already missed Liam and wondered if he was lying down with his leg up so it could finish healing.

Troy jumped at the sound of his cell phone ringing. He fished it out of his pocket and answered it without looking at the display.

"Troy?" He instantly recognized Jeanie's voice.

"Hi, Jeanie," Troy answered warily. "Is something wrong? Sofia's okay, isn't she?" A million things, all scary, flashed through his mind.

"Sofia's fine. She misses you." Jeanie sounded so tentative, which was quite unusual. Jeanie had always been a confident woman, and Troy knew he was the source of the insecurity in her life.

"She told me she hated me the last time I talked to her." Troy swallowed hard as his daughter's words rang in his ears one more time.

"She's five, and I was upset, so she was upset," Jeanie said defensively. "I really don't want to go into all that. I called for a reason and I need to get this out. You hurt me badly, Troy, but I think I'm beginning to understand. I'm not sure I'm ready to forgive, but I'm not mad at you anymore, either." Her voice trailed off, and Troy stopped himself from seizing on her words. They were very clearly a preamble to something, and he waited, knowing she'd get around to it when she was ready. "I think I need to speak with you face to face."

"Do you want me to come there?" Troy asked almost immediately.

"No. I think Sofia and I are going to come see you. If you come here, then I'm afraid she's going to think that you've come home and everything is going to be like it was. We both know that can't happen, and I think if she sees you in a different location with different people, that will be less likely to happen." That was Jeanie—always thinking about their daughter.

"That's fine. When are you going to come?"

"The sooner the better. I think we'll leave in a few days. I got the name of the town from Kevin, and I've made a reservation at a small hotel. But I think it might be good for Sofia to spend a few nights with you. She needs to know that you love her." Troy could barely keep himself under control at that point. Of course he loved his daughter. It hurt him all over again to think she didn't know that, and it hurt because he knew he was to blame. The doubt and guilt he'd been able to forget for a few days came roaring back to an almost debilitating degree.

"I do love her," Troy said weakly.

"I know you do. I didn't mean to insinuate that you don't, because I have no doubt that you do. She just needs to see it and feel your love again. I know this is going to be hard for you, and it's going to be hard for me, but we both need to work through things and we need closure.... I need closure." There was something in Jeanie's voice that made Troy stop and listen extra closely. "I need to be able to move on."

"Have you met someone?" Troy asked too quickly.

"I'm... I...," Jeanie stammered. "I don't know."

"I hope it works out for you...." Troy trailed off, partly because he didn't know what else to say, and partly because he wasn't sure if he should tell her about Liam. But Jeanie was too good at reading him.

"Have you?"

"I think I might have," Troy answered truthfully, and then he waited to see Jeanie's reaction.

"Is this serious?" she asked haltingly.

"I'm not sure about anything right now. I like Liam, I know that. But everything is still so muddled and confusing. Maybe, as you said, we need closure." Troy had no idea what else to say, and Jeanie didn't, either, because they both stayed quiet, waiting for the other to talk, and the silence quickly hung between them. "I'll see you in a few days," Troy said, finally breaking the quiet with expected phrases. "Call me when you get here, and I can meet you and bring you to the cabin." Jeanie agreed and then disconnected, leaving Troy to stare at the walls once again before finally springing into action. If Jeanie and Sofia were coming, he had plenty of things he needed to do and lots of nervous energy to work off.

Chapter Seven

LIAM wasn't sure about any of this. Troy had told him yesterday that his ex-wife and child were coming for a visit, and he really didn't know how he felt about all that. Troy had gone out of his way to assure him that both he and Jeanie needed closure, and Liam believed him. He knew how guilty Troy felt about the whole situation with them, and he hoped that maybe this would help Troy. But that worry was for tomorrow, when they were supposed to arrive. He had a different set of worries right now. Tonight was the council meeting, and Wally had said that he wanted everyone possible from the ranch to go.

Haven had been working at the ranch and worrying himself nearly to death. A few times, Liam had seen Phillip dragging his partner home during the workday, and when Haven returned, he always seemed more relaxed. "Some of the hands are going to watch things here," Dakota explained at the end of the workday. "Grace is coming over to sit with Dad, and the rest of us are going."

"Are you sure I should come?" Liam asked. "I've only been here a few weeks."

"You're a part of this community and the ranch, so we'd like you to come. The thing about these meetings is that numbers matter. The more people who show up to give their opinion, the better it gets heard. You don't have to speak; just being there is a help."

"Okay. But what if there's trouble?" Liam couldn't overcome the feeling that his father had opened all the doors on the ranch, and what if he did something worse next time?

"They'll call, and we'll be right back. The meeting starts at seven, and we'll take more than one vehicle, so if some of us need to come back, they can." Dakota smiled at him warmly. "Don't worry."

Liam nodded and then hurried inside to clean up and get ready. In the bathroom, he got undressed and hurriedly took a shower before putting on clean jeans and a nice shirt. When he was dressed, Liam went out to sit in the living room to wait for everyone else and was surprised to see Troy.

"Dakota asked me to come too," Troy said as an explanation, greeting Liam with a kiss.

Liam sat next to Troy on the sofa while they waited for the others. Once everyone was ready, they piled into the trucks, Liam riding with Troy, and headed for town.

The diner was packed when they arrived, but it seemed that Dakota had called ahead and a table in the back was waiting for them. "You going to the meeting?" their server, Denise, asked as she took their orders. "Everyone seems to be going."

"What's the lay of the land?" Dakota asked, and Denise chewed the end of her pencil lightly before answering.

"As you'd expect, I suppose. Some of the people in town think the mine will bring jobs and money, but others, like most of the ranchers, think the mine owners will bring in their own people and will leave nothing but a mess. Some don't care either way."

Dakota nodded his head like it was what he'd expected, and everyone placed their orders. Denise hurried away, returning with a tray of drinks and baskets of warm rolls. The conversation at the table centered around the meeting, but Liam paid more attention to Troy sitting right next to him than anyone else.

"By the way, Liam," Dakota said from next to Wally, "I passed those papers on to the lawyer. He'll call you in a few days."

"Thanks, Dakota," Liam responded, as one of his worries seemed to be handed off to someone else for the time being. They talked through dinner, and Liam did his best not to blush when he felt Troy take his hand under the table. They finished their meal and then walked over to the town hall, which seemed full to bursting with people. Liam knew almost none of them and stayed close to Wally and Troy as they managed to find seats near the back of the room. Others made their way inside, standing around the edges and even outside the room, in the hallway. A few people had signs, and Liam was pleased to see that they at least appeared to be against the mine. The room got quiet, and one of the men sitting behind the large desk up front called the meeting to order. Then everyone stood and recited the Pledge of Allegiance.

Afterward, the man spoke again and explained the proceedings for the evening. "I want to stress that we will not be making a decision this evening." The people from the mine, who sat together off to the side, dressed in suits, began whispering among themselves, not looking happy. "We are here to solicit public opinion, and everyone who wishes will get a chance to speak. First, we would like to give the representatives of Clayton Mining the chance to present their proposal, and then they have agreed to answer questions."

One of the men stood up and reviewed their proposal. They said they were looking for gold, and it appeared a potential vein had been located in the area they were leasing. "This will be a subterranean mine, and I want to stress that there will be no strip or placer mining done at the site. We have acquired a lease on the land and are in the process of finalizing our proposals with the US Department of the Interior. The one thing we do not have is access to a source of water, and that is where the good people of this community come in. We at Clayton Mining believe in being good citizens, as has already been demonstrated by our pledge to the community center. We firmly believe in being a part of the communities where we do business." He went on to explain just what they wanted to do and why. Liam didn't understand a lot of what the man was saying, especially when it came to land usability and access to water, but he thought the man sure made it sound like they had a right to the water in the first place.

Once he was done, a murmur went through the room, and rumbles of what sounded like discontent built. "Settle down," the man from the council—the chair, from what Liam had figured out—said, and the noise level quieted. "What we're going to do is open the floor for direct questions about the proposal."

To Liam's surprise, Dakota stood up and waited until he was called upon before saying his name for the record: "Dakota Holden." Liam saw him look around the room, and it appeared Dakota had plenty of support for whatever he wanted to say. "Based on what you've told us, I have a number of questions for you. Did I understand correctly that the amount of water you require will consume, when you're operating at peak capacity, between fifteen and twenty percent of the river's flow?"

"Yes, but only when we're operating," the man from the mining company answered.

"Which will be almost all the time," someone from the back said, and the chairman quieted everyone again.

"That means that in July, the river will be reduced to a trickle. The ranchers in the area will not have enough water to see us through the dry summer months," another man piped up.

Another murmur, louder this time, passed through the room like an ocean wave.

"Without the water, the lease we hold on the land isn't viable," the mining executive explained.

"Yes, and you should have thought of that before you leased land with no access to water," Dakota countered, and the murmurs changed to soft shows of support. "It is not the responsibility of the ranchers in this valley to pay for your self-imposed hardship." People in the back began to clap, and Dakota sat down.

Liam waited to see what would happen next, and a man he didn't recognize stood up and began asking questions as well. He was obviously a mine supporter, because his questions centered on jobs and revenue to the town. The meeting went on like that for quite a while, revealing two very obviously distinct camps. After a while, Dakota and Wally got up, as did the rest of the folks from the ranch, and headed out through the now thinning crowd.

"There's not going to be anything said that hasn't been heard before," Dakota explained, and he led the way to the exit and outside the building. "Let's head back to the ranch—we all have work to do in the morning. Nothing is going to be decided tonight." Everyone else agreed, and they walked back through town to where they'd parked their trucks. No one spoke at all, expressions of worry on everyone's faces, including Wally's and Troy's, which worried Liam most of all.

The ride in the truck was nearly silent, with just the sound of the road under the tires. "Can they just do that? Take all the water that the ranch needs?" Liam asked as he looked out the window. He thought he'd found a home, and it looked like these mining people were trying to take it away. Liam wasn't really expecting an answer, and Troy didn't try to give him one. When they arrived at the ranch, Liam walked around back and made sure the cats were all set before returning to the house, where everyone was sitting in the living room looking at each other, a bit stunned. Liam sat next to Troy and looked from person to person.

"Don't they need some sort of environmental impact study or something?" Haven asked, looking at Dakota.

"I asked the lawyer, and he said that since they're leasing rights from an existing holder, as opposed to trying to establish new rights, they didn't need one, which is a shame, because those studies are expensive and can take years. The study may not stop them, but it would certainly slow the process down."

"What are we going to do?" Liam asked, and Wally shrugged.

"Go to bed," Dakota answered. "We're all tired and not thinking clearly." He got up and took Wally's hand, leading him down the hallway. Haven and Phillip left as well, closing the door quietly on their way out. Liam didn't want Troy to leave, and when Troy got up, Liam took his hand the way Dakota had taken Wally's and led him down the hall. They simply undressed and climbed into bed, and Troy held him tight. Liam rested his head on the pillow, feeling Troy slide his hand slowly up and down his arm as Troy's body pressed to his back.

"I'm sorry," Liam said softly.

"What for?" Troy asked, stopping his hand.

"I'm not up to… stuff tonight." Liam could feel that Troy seemed to be.

A kiss lightly touched Liam's shoulder. "It has a mind of its own, especially when I'm around you." Troy yawned and tugged Liam closer, and Liam closed his eyes, wishing he could turn off the worry.

"What if we can't stop these guys? It could ruin the ranch."

"We will," Troy said, but Liam could hear he wasn't convinced. "Somehow we'll stop them and convince people of the impact. It'll take some time. Go to sleep. Worrying won't change things, and you'll just be tired in the morning." Liam agreed and closed his eyes, trying his best to fall asleep, but even the normal sounds of the ranch through the open window didn't seem to soothe him.

"What was that?" Troy asked a while later, sitting up in bed, and Liam jerked awake after finally having drifted off.

"A wolf, I think. Wally said they sometimes hear them when they wander down out of the national parks," Liam explained, and then Manny let loose a roar that echoed off the hills.

"So this is part of their territory," Troy stated, and Liam waited for him to settle back into bed. They heard no more cries, and eventually Liam fell asleep.

Liam woke to Troy getting out of bed. "Is something wrong?" Liam asked, and Troy leaned over the mattress, kissing him sweetly.

"No, not at all," he answered with a hint of excitement in his voice. "I need to make a few phone calls." Troy finished dressing and then left the room. Liam settled back under the covers and promptly fell back to sleep, but woke when Troy came back into the room later. "Are you going to get up? I think there are some cats ready for their breakfast."

"Did you make your calls?" Liam asked, yawning.

"Yes, but I'm not sure they'll come to anything." Troy seemed nervous, and the earlier excitement was gone. "Jeanie and Sofia are coming today...."

"I know," Liam answered. He hadn't really expected to meet them, although Liam was curious what Troy's ex-wife was like. They talked a little bit, and Liam expected he wouldn't see Troy very much until Jeanie and Sofia left. Troy moved close to the bed, and Liam was about to push back the covers to get up when Troy's arms wrapped around him, tugging him close before kissing him hard.

"I needed that," Troy said when their lips parted. "I'm really nervous."

"You shouldn't be. Jeanie called you—this was her idea. I think that's a good thing. It probably means that she's beginning to move on, something that maybe both of you need." God, Liam hoped that was true. Troy needed to shed some of the guilt he was feeling. Liam knew he was fast developing feelings for Troy, but he wasn't sure there was any chance for him as long as Troy felt guilty and couldn't move on from his past.

"But I am nervous. I love Sofia, but what if she won't have anything to do with me? And then there's Jeanie. I have no idea how I'm going to feel when I see her. Hell, she may haul off and slug me, not that I could blame her."

"Would you stop that?" Liam said as he pushed past Troy and got out of bed. "Yes, you hurt them, but wallowing in your own feelings like some sort of martyr isn't going to help you or them. You covered up who you were for a long time. So what? People used to do it their entire lives for fear they'd be killed. In the end, you were honest, and it hurt, but in the long run, they'll be better off and so will you. Go make peace with them."

"That sounds like Wally talking," Troy accused, and Liam crossed his arms over his chest, forgetting he was naked.

"So? He's smart." Troy chuckled, and Liam scowled. "What's so funny?" Liam demanded.

"That look would work better if you weren't naked." Troy's laughter trailed off as Liam looked down at himself and realized that Troy was probably right.

"That doesn't mean I'm wrong," Liam countered.

"No, it doesn't." Troy slid his hands around Liam's waist, and he tugged Liam closer, resting his head against Liam's belly. "Not at all."

Certain parts of Liam's anatomy were definitely taking an interest in Troy's closeness, and he heard another chuckle and felt Troy gently cup his balls in one hand. Liam's breath hitched, and he stood still, waiting to see what Troy would do next.

A knock on the door made Liam jump, and he pulled away before searching around for his clothes. "Liam, are you up?"

"Yes, Wally. I'll be right out," Liam called through the door, and he heard Wally's laughter fade as he moved down the hall. "See what you made me do. I'm going to be late for work, and Wally's gonna be mad at me." Liam continued dressing, but he wasn't really mad, and when he smiled at Troy, he saw the other man return it. They shared another quick kiss before Liam hurried out of the room with Troy behind him. They said their good-byes, and Liam wished his lover luck before hurrying outside to begin his chores.

Liam kept himself busy, but many times through the morning, he wondered how things were going for Troy. His leg felt a lot better, so he helped in the barn once he was done with his other chores, only stopping for lunch.

"Liam, I got a call from the lawyer, and he wants to speak with you." Dakota looked concerned. "Could you come into the office? He's going to call us back in just a few minutes."

Liam put his tools away before following Dakota inside the small room with a desk that was as neat as a pin. Usually, this was where Phillip worked, and it appeared the man was extremely particular about his work area. Liam sat down in one of the chairs just as the phone rang. Dakota answered it and put it on speaker. "Liam, this is John Fabian, who reviewed the papers your father gave you."

"Hello, Liam," John said. "Is Dakota still there?"

"Yes," Liam answered.

"Do you want him to stay?" John asked, and Dakota got up from behind the desk and walked toward the door.

"Yes," Liam answered, wondering just what was going on. He really wished Troy were here for support, too, because he figured whatever news he was going to get was bad.

"Okay. I have to ask because of client confidentiality," John explained, and Dakota sat back down. "I looked over these papers, and at first I couldn't figure out why your father would want you to sign papers for the sale of his ranch. What I've determined as the reason is that it's not his ranch. It took a great deal of digging, but it appears that the ranch was your grandfather's, and he died when you were small, leaving half of it to you and half to your mother. Your portion was left in trust with your parents as trustees. It appears that your mother signed over the property to the trust years ago. It was hard to find details, but I managed, and it seems that while you're not of age to receive the trust yet, since you've turned eighteen, your approval is required to make any major changes in trust assets. And selling the ranch is a major change."

"Why would he do that?" Liam asked. His confusion had his head spinning, but the line remained silent. Lifting his gaze from the desk, Liam looked at Dakota, and he knew, because he could read on Dakota's face that he knew as well. "He wanted to steal from me, didn't he?"

"I don't know your father from Adam, but it looks as though that's a possibility. He could say that he was withdrawing money to cover his maintenance of the trust, and since it doesn't mature until you're twenty-five, there might not be much money left."

"What do I do?" Liam felt totally helpless, just like he always had at the hands of his father.

"For now, nothing. Let me dig further and explore some options," John advised him, and Liam looked at Dakota, who nodded, so Liam agreed. After a few pleasantries, they disconnected, and Liam stared at Dakota, unable to believe what he'd heard.

"Would he do that?" Liam asked, not expecting Dakota to answer. "Yeah, he would, the old bastard," Liam answered his own question before getting up. "Thanks, Dakota."

"You're welcome, and John will find an answer, don't worry." Liam knew Dakota was trying to be reassuring, but he wasn't worried about the money.

"It's not that. It's finding out just how greedy and hateful my father can be. Sometimes I used to think I was to blame for the way my father treated me. I knew I was a disappointment to him." Liam's hand shook as he reached for the door. "I'm not sure what hurts worse, thinking my father was going to steal from me, or him thinking I wasn't smart enough to find out." Liam turned the knob and left the office, nearly walking into Wally as he hurried down the hallway in his rush to get outside and into the fresh air.

"Is everything okay?" Wally asked, and Liam shook his head, not trusting himself to speak at that moment. "Troy called and he asked you to call him back. You left your phone on the counter," Wally added as an explanation before heading down the hallway toward the office.

Liam didn't watch him go. Instead he picked up his phone to call Troy, wondering if something was wrong. God, he hoped not. Pressing the buttons, he waited for the call to connect. "Troy?"

"Liam, you got my message."

"Yeah. Wally just told me."

"What's wrong?" Troy asked immediately. "You don't sound so good."

"I just spoke with the lawyer about those papers from my dad." Liam swallowed and stopped, getting himself under control. "I'm okay. Is there something you needed?"

"Jeanie and Sofia arrived, and Jeanie asked if she could meet you." Troy sounded excited, but Liam thought he was about to be sick. This was too much, and Liam's hand shook as he stared at the phone display before disconnecting the call. There was no way he could meet Troy's ex-wife, not now. Liam made his way to the living room and flopped into one of the chairs, putting his head between his knees.

"It's okay, Liam," Wally said quietly from behind him. He hadn't even heard his footsteps. "Just relax and breathe. Dakota told me what happened, and if I see your father again, more than his butt will be bouncing in the dirt."

Liam would have laughed, but he was having trouble breathing. He felt Wally's hand on his back, rubbing lightly and slowly. Carefully, Liam pulled in a breath, hoping it wouldn't cause him to throw up.

Thankfully it didn't, and slowly the room stopped spinning and his double vision returned to normal. "I'm okay," Liam said softly between breaths.

"Take it easy," Wally said as a loud knock came from the front door. "I'll answer it. You going to be okay?" Liam nodded, and he heard the front door open, and then Troy's voice followed by rapid footsteps.

"Are you okay?" Troy said from next to him as he took his hand. "When you just hung up without saying anything, I got worried that something was wrong and rushed down."

"I'm okay. I guess I got a bit overwrought." Liam took a deep breath, checking the tightness in his chest, which seemed to have abated as well.

"I'm sorry I shocked you," Troy said, holding him lightly.

"It wasn't that. Well, it wasn't only that." Liam breathed regularly and carefully, glad whatever had happened to him seemed to be over. "I think I'm okay now." Liam carefully sat upright before leaning back in the chair. "Too many surprises all at once," Liam said, hoping that was the reason for all his weird feelings. "That's never happened before." *Thankfully*, and he hoped it never happened again.

"I'm sorry for being so careless," Troy continued, holding his hand as Liam felt his heart rate return to normal and the sweat that had broken out all over him began to cool. "Do you need a drink of water?" Liam shook his head and continued breathing regularly, closing his eyes and letting everything settle back down.

"You just gave me a bit of a shock, that's all." Liam wanted to explain that it probably had been the stuff with his dad that had been the actual cause, but he didn't feel up to it right now. All he wanted to do was go someplace quiet and dark and hide for a while. "I'll be all right. I promise. You should get back to Jeanie and Sofia before they wonder what happened to you." Liam didn't want everyone hovering over him; it made him self-conscious, and he needed room to breathe. "What?" he asked when he saw Troy chewing on his lower lip. "What's going on?"

"When you called we were on our way to town," Troy explained.

"We?" Liam asked as what Troy had said dawned on him. "They're here with you?" Liam felt his chest tighten again, and he closed his eyes, trying to make the pounding stop. He wasn't really sure why he was reacting this way.

"Yes. She and Sofia are in the truck." Troy sounded worried and conflicted. "I don't want to leave you while you're feeling like this."

Liam opened his eyes, looking intently at Troy. "I promise to meet them if you want me to before they leave. And when we're alone, I'll tell you what's going on, but you need to spend time with them and work things out." Liam breathed steadily as he tried not to let his worries run away with him. Troy squeezed his hand, and Liam felt him lightly kiss his cheek before leaving the room. Liam saw Troy stop at the door, looking back at him worriedly before opening it to leave.

Once he was gone, Liam could breathe better, and some of the anxiety left him, only to be replaced with new worries. "Are you okay with all this?" Wally asked.

"Yes… no… I have no idea," Liam answered. "I know that Troy needs to make peace with Jeanie and Sofia, for his own good. He's carrying a lot of guilt and hurt around with him, and he needs to be able to let some of it go. I know that." Liam took another deep breath and relaxed back into the chair.

"Then what has you so worried?" Wally asked, and Liam watched him sit down on the sofa across from him.

Liam took another deep breath and slowly released it. "Troy's cabin isn't suitable for winter, and if he makes peace with Jeanie and Sofia, I guess I'm worried that he'll move back east. I can't blame him for wanting to be close to his daughter." Now that he'd started, Liam couldn't seem to stop everything from tumbling out. "He deserves to be close to Sofia, and she deserves to have her father in her life. Troy's a great person and he'll make a good dad. Definitely worlds better than the father I ended up with." Liam couldn't help taking a stab at the bastard. "But I don't want him to go. I want him to stay here." He left off the "with me" part because Liam figured it would make him seem too needy, but Wally knew exactly what he meant, Liam could see it on his face.

"I know what you're feeling, and if I could tell you everything would be all right I would, but I can't. I know you care for Troy, it's plain whenever you look at him, and I think he feels the same way. Have you asked him what he's planning?"

Liam shook his head. "I want him to be able to make his own decision. He feels guilty enough about how he treated Jeanie and Sofia. I don't want to add to that."

"Liam, sweetheart…." Wally was off the sofa and Liam was being hugged in a matter of seconds. "I wish there was something I could do."

Wally continued hugging him. "What's all this about promising to meet Troy's ex-wife?"

Liam relaxed into Wally's comforting arms. "She apparently wants to meet me. And while I'll admit I'm curious about her and Sofia, I don't know how I feel about the whole thing. It seems kind of weird."

Wally was quiet for a long time, and after a while, Wally's arms slipped away, and he returned to the sofa, looking as though he were deep in thought. "I can see where it would seem weird, but maybe it's not such a bad thing after all. Troy wants you to meet her. It isn't like he's acting as though you're some dirty little secret or someone he's seeing on the sly. He's being honest with her, with you, and with himself. That can't be a bad thing for either of you."

"But what if he moves to be closer to his daughter?" Liam tried to keep at least some of his fear out of his voice.

Wally shrugged. "When things seem overwhelming for me, I take it one day at a time. There are a lot of things going on right now, and that's all we can do." Wally stood up, and Liam felt him pat his knee. "Relax and take it easy for a while. I have some things to do and some farm calls to make. I'll see you later. Promise me you won't just worry about this."

Liam nodded his head slowly and waited until Wally was gone before cautiously getting to his feet and wandering out back to where the cats were lounging in the sun. Manny barely lifted his head as Liam approached, his tail flicking the grass. Liam made sure they all had water before wandering over to the barns, wondering what else could happen.

Chapter Eight

TROY left Liam in the house and walked to his truck, knowing there were two sets of eyes watching his every move. Opening the door, both sets of eyes shifted toward him as Troy got inside and closed the door. "Is he okay?" Jeanie asked.

"Yes. I think he got a bit of a shock. It wasn't you, though. He said something about his father."

"You could take Sofia and me back to the hotel if you need to," Jeanie said. Both he and Jeanie had been on edge since he'd picked them up at the hotel. He'd shown them both the cabin, and then Liam had called just as they were heading to town to get something to eat.

"It's all right," Troy said levelly. "What would you like to eat, honey?" Troy asked Sofia.

"Nuggets, Daddy," she answered, and Troy felt his heart soar. She hadn't said anything at all to him up to now. Since he'd seen her, she'd clung to her mother and not said a word to Troy. A few times she'd whispered answers to his questions to Jeanie, but other than that, she'd simply looked at him with wide eyes, like he was a stranger.

"Okay, nuggets it is. I think the diner in town has what you want. There's no McDonald's here. Is that okay?" Troy asked, and she nodded. Troy drove the rest of the way back into town without much conversation from any of them. Troy parked in front of the small restaurant and waited for Jeanie to go in first. On the sidewalk, Troy reached out to take Sofia's hand like he'd always done before, and she moved away, reaching for Jeanie's hand instead. Troy should have expected that, but it still hurt.

Jeanie, bless her heart, mouthed, "Give her time," before pulling open the door and going inside. Troy had known this was going to be hard, but reality appeared to be making that an understatement.

The hostess led them to a small table, and Sofia sat next to Jeanie, with Troy across the table. "So," Jeanie started once they had their menus. "How are you really?"

"Messed up," were the first words out of his mouth, and he wished he could take them back as soon as he'd said them.

"Mommy, I have to go," Sofia said, sliding under the table.

"Do you want me to take you?" Jeanie asked, and Sofia rolled her eyes.

"I'm not a baby." Both of them watched as Sofia walked confidently toward the bathroom. Jeanie turned back to him, but Troy knew she still had one eye on the bathroom.

"I know the feeling. But I've had time to think and I hope I've realized something. No, Troy," she added when he opened his mouth, "please let me get this out all at once." Troy closed his mouth and girded himself for a lambasting. "We were married for six years, and mostly they were happy. We were happy, or at least I thought we were, though I realized something. For the last few years, we've been more like friends who lived together and had a daughter than anything else. Other couples take vacations alone; we never did. Both our lives were busy, and I think we were using that as cover."

"What is it you're trying to say?" Troy asked softly.

Jeanie gulped from her water. "I've been talking to your brother, Kevin, a lot lately, and he's been...." Jeanie shook her head and took another drink of her water. "He's been amazing. He's tried to explain things as best he could, and he's been there for both of us a lot. He made me realize that while you'd been hiding yourself from us, you'd also been hiding from yourself. As I said on the phone, I'm beginning to understand and even forgive. I was hurt terribly when you told me, but I realize now that you were hurting just as much as I was, and maybe it's time we figured out how to live with each other for both our sakes and Sofia's."

"What are you saying? That you want me to come back?" Troy asked skeptically. He doubted that was it, but that was the only idea that he could get from her statement.

"In a manner of speaking. I think we both need you in our lives. For me as a friend, and for Sofia as a father. This last year has been hard on all of us, and I don't think any of us should go on as we have."

"So what are you proposing?" Troy could hardly believe his ears.

"I don't know where you are going to live, but if you're going to stay here, then you should come back east a few weeks a year, and Sofia will come here for part of her summers. We can work through holidays and things. You need to be in each other's lives."

"I thought I'd ruined any possibility of that," Troy said as he broke into a smile. "This is more than I dreamed. Can I ask what brought this about?"

"In part, Kevin, and in part, your own actions. When we separated, I didn't realize until recently just what you'd done to make sure Sofia and I were taken care of. I was too upset and angry to comprehend just what a wonderful, giving thing you'd done. You took nothing at all from our relationship and gave up what you received from your parents so Sofia and I could be taken care of. Few people would have seen to that, but you did."

"You were my wife, and she's my daughter. There was nothing else for me to do," Troy said honestly, and Jeanie nodded knowingly. Jeanie turned toward the bathroom as Sofia walked back toward the table.

"And that's why we're here," Jeanie added before letting Sofia take her seat. Once she was seated, Jeanie leaned down to Sofia and said something in her ear that Troy couldn't hear.

"But Daddy made you cry, Mommy," Sofia said.

"I know, but Daddy's sorry," Jeanie said, alternately looking at Sofia and then Troy.

"It's okay," Troy said. "I need to give her time." That was the hardest thing he'd ever had to do in his life, but Troy knew he had to be patient and let things happen on Sofia's time. If he was to have a chance with her, things had to happen at her pace.

The server stopped at the table, and they ordered drinks and food. "Sofia, was the trip in the plane fun?"

"Yes. Mommy let me sit next to the window," Sofia said with a slight smile on her tiny face. Troy hated how quiet she'd become, and how guarded. She was five years old, and over the past few months, it seemed like she'd aged a lot.

"Did you see fun stuff from the air?"

"Clouds and stuff," Sofia answered softly, almost like Troy was a stranger. "It was fun until I started feeling woofy. But Mommy gave me these awful pink pills to eat and I felt better."

"Do you still like school?"

"Yes. I'm in the same room as Callie and Ruthie." Sofia sounded a little excited, and Troy felt pleased that she wasn't just sitting there watching him like before. "Daddy, at that place where we stopped, they had horses."

"Would you like to see the horses up close? I can ask to see if that would be okay." He knew Wally and Dakota would probably let him show Sofia all around the ranch. "Wally, he's a vet, has some special animals out back, and I bet he would show them to you too. I'll ask if you can see the horses."

Sofia smiled, and their drinks arrived, followed by the food. Sofia talked through their meal, asking all kinds of questions about the horses. Troy knew very little, but answered her questions patiently, pleased that she was talking to him about something. Even Jeanie seemed interested, and by the time they were done eating, Troy had relaxed and begun to feel as though the weight he'd been feeling on his shoulders for months was beginning to lift.

"Would you like me to take you back to the hotel?" Troy asked when they left the diner.

"Yes, please. They have a pool where Sofia can go swimming. We'll call you in the morning. Maybe we could go to one of the parks for the day," Jeanie said, and while Troy had hoped they could all go back to the cabin, he didn't want to push. Everything had gone better than he could possibly have hoped, so after he took them to the hotel, Troy headed toward home, stopping first at the ranch before heading up the hill, since he was concerned about Liam.

At the ranch, he found Liam feeding the cats their dinner. "Are you feeling better?" Troy asked as he approached, so he wouldn't startle Liam.

Liam paused in what he was doing. "Yes. How did it go with Jeanie and Sofia?"

"Better than I could possibly have hoped. When you're finished here, I'll tell you all about it." Troy was so excited he couldn't wait to tell Liam all about it. Liam nodded, and Troy stepped back and let Liam finish his chores without his interference before following him back toward the ranch house. Seated in the living room, Troy excitedly told Liam what Jeanie had said. "It isn't perfect, but it seems as though we've made a start." The relief and hope that Troy felt while listening to Jeanie bloomed into full-fledged joy as he talked to Liam.

Troy expected Liam to be happy for him, but what he saw in his face was more of the anxiety from earlier in the day. "It sounds as though you've gotten everything you could want, and that's wonderful. I really am happy for you." Liam got up and slowly walked to the front windows, gazing out over the yard. "When are you leaving to go back home? I assume that you'll want to be near Sofia. Not that I can blame you. She deserves your time. She's your daughter and she needs you."

All Troy could see was Liam's back, but the tone of his voice and the uncomfortable way he shifted from foot to foot told Troy everything he needed to know about how Liam was feeling. "I'm going to stay here." Troy stood and joined Liam, sliding his arms around the other man's waist. "Don't you know that what happened today would not have been possible without you? I was dead inside, and you've helped bring me back to where I can feel again. I was so filled with shame that I couldn't see anything beyond myself, and you changed that." Troy spun Liam in his arms. "You showed me that there was someone who cared about me. I saw it in your face when you looked at me and in your eyes when we made love."

"I didn't do anything," Liam protested lightly.

"Yes, you did, and I love you more than I can possibly say for it." There, Troy had actually said what was in his heart as opposed to hiding with shame and cowardice. Damned if it didn't feel good, and the expression on Liam's face was worth every bit of anxiety he'd felt since he'd first realized weeks ago what his feelings were.

"Is that true?" Liam lifted his eyes to see Troy's, their blue now shockingly deep and rich. "Do you love me?"

"Yes," Troy answered softly, and he couldn't help thinking of the last time he'd said those words to someone. This time, however, there was no trepidation or fear inside. "I do. I never thought I could love anyone; I didn't think I was capable of it anymore." Troy's heart pounded in his chest at the thought of what he'd just said. "I want to stay here. I like it here, and I like the people here. They're kind and supportive, and they're *real*. I sort of feel like I've found a home." Troy trailed off as he waited for Liam to say something. He'd been doing almost all the talking, and he needed to know how Liam felt, even though he could pretty much see it in his eyes, in the way they danced, and in the smile that threatened on Liam's lips just before he must have realized he couldn't keep it inside any longer.

"Are you staying for me?" Liam asked, after a huge swallow. "Because that wouldn't be right." Troy could see fear tinged with hope and longing in Liam's eyes.

"No. I'm staying for me, and to be with you. There's a difference, I guess. I think I'd want to be here even if you weren't." Troy squeezed Liam closer. "But you make it better here."

"What about Sofia? She deserves to be with you," Liam asked, his head resting on Troy's shoulder, and it felt right.

"She will. I'll go back and see her, and she'll come out here to see me," Troy answered.

"But what about…," Liam began, and Troy pulled away from him and kissed the words from Liam's lips. He'd meant the kiss to be gentle, just something to quell the questions and to reinforce to Liam just how he felt, but it quickly deepened into more. Troy felt Liam open his mouth, and Troy's tongue slid inside, tasting and dueling a little with Liam's. A small moan began deep in Liam's throat, and Troy kissed him harder, pulling out those sounds he loved so much.

"Troy," Liam said, pulling back and breathing hard. "We shouldn't do this here." The words were barely out of Liam's mouth before Troy had him by the hand, leading them through the house to Liam's bedroom. Closing the door with his foot, Troy pulled Liam close once again. "Troy, please stop."

Troy froze, looking deeply into Liam's eyes and seeing something he didn't expect—insecurity and doubt. "What's bothering you?"

"Troy, this is too much. Your ex-wife and daughter are in town, my father's causing trouble, this whole water thing with the ranch. It's becoming more than I can take." Liam sat on the edge of the bed, and Troy sat next to him, taking Liam's hand.

"I'm sorry, I should have been thinking of more than just myself. I was happy about what Jeanie said, and I assumed you would be too."

"I am. I'm happy that things are working out for you, and I'm happy that you want to stay." Liam shifted on the bed. "I really am. It's just that with everything that's going on, I'm having trouble getting my head around everything." Liam took a deep breath. "I think my dad's the one who opened all the gates, and Dakota's lawyer thinks he's trying to pull something with the ranch back in Texas. I just don't know what to do with any of it."

"Hey." Troy touched Liam's arm softly. "Let's take it one step at a time. You aren't alone anymore. That is, if you don't want to be. You have Wally and Dakota to help, and me, if you'll let me." Troy waited to see Liam's reaction, and Liam slowly looked at him, examining his face as though he could hardly believe what Troy was saying. "I love you and I'll help you, just like you helped me."

"Wally said to take it one day at a time, but that keeps getting harder." Liam seemed frazzled, so Troy put his arms around him.

"You don't have to take the weight of the world. So, let's pick one, okay? It sounds as though Dakota's attorney has things in hand with what's happening at the ranch. Do you want to talk about it?"

"There's not much to say other than my bastard father is being true to form. But there's nothing I can do about that…."

"Just like there's nothing you can do about your father opening the gates. That is, if he did it, and for the record I think he did, as well. Do you know if Dakota or Wally reported it?" Troy asked, and Liam shook his head.

"But the bastard is making trouble for them because of me." Liam's shoulders slumped as more of the energy and spunk seemed to drain from him.

"That's your father talking. I know, because I used to feel the same way whenever something went wrong."

"What did you do?"

"Treated everyone like dirt and acted like a complete shit. That way no one would press unless they wanted a real fight, and in my family they never did." Troy realized that once again he'd brought the conversation back to him. "You are not responsible for your father and the way he acts. Only he is. When was Dakota's lawyer supposed to get back to you?'

"In a couple of days."

"When he does, ask him what you should do about your father. I suggest you tell him everything, if you feel up to it. I'll be there with you if you want, but he needs to know it all," Troy suggested, and Liam nodded, but didn't look happy about it. "There's one thing I've learned from all those years working in government: you can't fight with what you don't know. Knowledge is power, so tell the attorney everything and let him help you."

"What about your family?"

"Jeanie does want to meet you. I think she's curious, but if you don't feel up to it, I'll tell her that you can't." Troy smiled, adding, "Though I'd really like you to meet Sofia."

"Will she like me?" Liam asked in a soft voice.

"I think they both will. But I know Sofia will be thrilled if you were to take her on a special tour to see the animals. She was only here a few minutes and has already asked if she could come see the horses." Troy thought for a while. "Jeanie seemed to have let go of a lot of the hurt and animosity she was carrying, and in turn I've been able to ease up on some of the guilt. Both of us have begun to realize that we each deserve to be happy. I hope she finds someone, because I think I have," Troy said, noticing that Liam hadn't said anything to him about how he felt. Not that it was necessary, but….

"You really think that?"

"Why is that so hard for you to believe?" Troy asked, and Liam smiled slightly.

"I believe you. It's just nice to hear it. I haven't in a very long time, and I'm not used to telling other people how I feel, either. Dad always said it was weak and girly. I guess he was full of crap in so many ways." Liam leaned closer as they hugged each other in the quiet room. Until that moment, Troy had not realized just how intimate and close two people could be, and it didn't involve getting naked or sex, just two people being honest about how they felt. "I don't know if I really know what it means to love someone, but that's what I feel for you. I know that sounds kind of dumb."

"No. It's honest," Troy said. He'd take Liam's honesty over flowery sentiment or Liam telling him what he wanted to hear.

Liam smiled mischievously. "So, since we've talked about my dad, and your ex-wife and daughter—"

"You still haven't said if you'll meet them," Troy interrupted, and this time Liam didn't falter.

"If you're there, I'll meet them. I don't know what good it will do, but I'll admit to being slightly curious." Troy felt Liam place a finger over his lips. "Now, as I was saying, all we need to do now is solve the problem of this mining company taking all the water."

Troy waited, keeping his lips tightly closed until Liam chuckled and removed his finger. "I have an idea about that, but we need to speak with Wally and Dakota. I'm not saying it'll work, and it may not stop the mining company, but it could slow them to a crawl and maybe discourage them from doing anything at all." Troy angled his face closer to Liam's. "Now that we've solved the problems of the world," Troy said as he touched his lips to Liam's, "I'd like to show my lover just how much I love him. And afterward, maybe we can solve the rest of the world's problems. But…." Troy stopped moving. "If you aren't up to doing anything, it's okay. I just want to be with you."

Liam smiled and pressed against him, kissing through his smile. Troy found himself falling backward as he returned Liam's laugh, wrapping his arms around Liam and pulling him down on top of him. Their smiles faded as the intensity of their kisses increased, the small chuckles replaced with soft moans. Liam's weight settled on top of him, and Troy relished it, guiding Liam's face to his for yet another kiss that seemed to go on and on.

"Liam, I love you," Troy gasped between kisses as he did his best to work off Liam's clothes. Somehow, he managed to get Liam's shirt off, their kiss breaking only long enough for him to pull Liam's shirt over his head. Troy got his shirt off, as well, and then he and Liam were skin to skin. Troy loved Liam's touch, and his lover's chest pressing against his felt amazing, especially since he could feel each breath Liam took and each and every quiver of his body. "I want you, Liam. I want to feel you inside me."

Liam stopped, his gaze drilling into Troy's, his lower lip slipping between his teeth. "I've never...." Liam's voice trailed off, and he swallowed hard. "I...."

"It's okay, Liam. You won't hurt me, I promise." Troy turned them on the bed, kissing Liam once more before lifting his body and helping his lover get comfortable. Before climbing back on the bed, Troy shucked the rest of his clothes, watching as Liam did the same. He might have been inexperienced with true intimacy, but Liam's body seemed ready and willing. "You're incredible," Troy soothed softly, reaching out a hand, stroking along Liam's length.

"Troy," Liam whined softly, his hips flexing slightly.

"I want you, Liam. I want to feel you, and I want you to know how you make me feel," Troy whispered softly as he climbed back onto the bed. As soon as he held Liam once again, Liam turned them and was soon staring down at him. Troy had already found that Liam had more dominant tendencies in the bedroom, and that was just fine with him. Troy liked that Liam could be strong and commanding.

He wrapped his legs around Liam's waist, and they kissed themselves breathless. "Do you have any condoms?" Liam shook his head, and Troy smiled, trying to remember if he had any. Pointing to his pants, he felt Liam's weight shift off him. "There's one in my wallet. It hasn't been there very long."

"Hopeful, were you?" Liam teased as he fished the billfold out of Troy's back pocket and found the foil packet.

"I've been hopeful around you almost since we met," Troy responded as Liam leapt back onto the bed, enthusiastically bounding back on top of Troy. "You need to get me ready for you," Troy explained softly, not wanting to break the mood. "Use your fingers."

"Like this?" Liam asked, sliding two fingers between Troy's lips before reaching beneath him and teasing the skin at his entrance, slowly working one into Troy's body.

"Yes," Troy answered, throwing his head back when Liam hit that magic spot right away. He'd expected some fumbling, but Liam had zeroed in on the spot in two seconds flat. Once he could catch his breath, Troy caught Liam's eyes. "How?"

"I have one too, you know," Liam said, and Troy thought his head would explode. The image of Liam with his fingers buried inside himself, exploring his own body, was almost enough to make Troy come right then and there. And before he could think, Liam stroked deep into his body, and rational thought about Liam or anything else flew from his head.

"Oh my God!" Troy intoned as a second finger joined the first. The slight burn was exquisite, and Troy hoped it would never stop. Then Liam's fingers slipped away, and Troy wanted to ask what happened. Troy lifted his head and his eyes grew wide as he watched Liam open the condom packet and then, in an unsure manner, roll the condom down his length. "It feels funny," he said with a smile that quickly faded, his eyes darkening as he met Troy's gaze.

"Go slowly," Troy reminded him as Liam pressed to his entrance. Troy's body resisted at first, but then opened, and Liam slid inside. Troy hissed softly at the stretch and burn, and Liam stopped, widening his eyes, and Troy felt him begin to pull back out. "It's okay. Just give me a minute," Troy cautioned, willing his body to relax.

"I can feel you," Liam whispered with a touch of awe in his voice. "It's like I'm a part of you." Liam pressed deeper, going quite slowly, and Troy tried to catch his breath as he, too, felt the connection between them. Once Troy felt Liam's hips against his butt, he breathed a quiet sigh and held Liam's leg in a signal not to move. Troy closed his eyes and simply enjoyed the feeling of Liam buried deep within him.

"Your heart's racing," Liam said, and Troy smiled. It was, and that was the amazing thing about this type of connection—you could feel the other person, especially if you were paying attention. Troy had only felt it once before, and that was with Jeanie. He'd had anonymous sex, and it felt nothing like this. Not even close.

"It is," Troy agreed, and he patted Liam's leg. Slowly, Liam began to move, drawing himself out before pressing back into Troy's body.

"God, Troy, does it always feel like this?" Liam gasped, and Troy tightened his muscles, earning a surprised gasp from Liam. "Do that again," Liam said as he stopped. Troy tightened his muscles around Liam and held them, squeezing his shaft, and he saw Liam's eyes close as he gasped once again. When Troy released his muscles, Liam leaned over him, kissing him hard, possessively. "I haven't had much in my life that I can truly call my own."

Troy smiled and nodded, knowing the implication of what Liam was saying. "I love you," Troy responded, and Liam took his hands, placing them over his head, stretching Troy out on the bed.

"I love you too," Liam said, snapping his hips as he said it, and Troy gasped, both from the words and from the sensation that zinged along his spine. "You look," Liam began, seeming to be searching for the word he wanted, "decadent, all laid out for me." Liam began thrusting faster, and Troy tried not to close his eyes. He wanted to see Liam and watch the joy on his face, but the man was driving him crazy. It wasn't perfect, and of course there was a certain amount of fumbling, but Troy barely noticed it. All he saw was the way Liam's eyes glowed and the way his body glistened with sweat. And all he felt was what Liam made him feel, as though he were the most important person in the world.

Liam gripped Troy's hips, thrusting deeper and harder.

"That's it, Liam, show me what you're feeling," Troy encouraged.

"I love you," Liam said, driving deep, and Troy gasped, his back arching into the torrents of passion that washed through him. Troy felt Liam's fingers digging into his side as he steadied himself. He'd probably have marks, but he didn't care. All that mattered to him was the way Liam looked at him and the way Troy felt his heart expand every time Liam moved.

Liam must have realized how hard he was gripping because he rubbed Troy's side before stroking his hands over Troy's chest and then down his stomach, gripping him tightly. Troy left his hands over his head and let Liam control the pleasure for both of them. The man was a natural, driving Troy mad with every touch.

Troy wanted to thrust into Liam's grip, but cried out in passionate frustration when Liam drove inside him and held still.

"I'll take care of you, I promise," Liam said softly before giving Troy the fucking of his life. He'd asked Liam to show him what he was feeling, and Liam was doing just that. Sweat glistened off Liam's lithe body, running down his chest, and still he continued. Finally, Liam gave him what he really wanted and began stroking Troy in earnest. It didn't take long for Troy to feel the familiar tightness in his groin and warmth in his belly. His body tightened, and Troy heard Liam gasp as his release built and built. Troy could barely think or breathe as Liam kept from giving him that little bit he needed, keeping him hanging on the edge. Troy figured it was accidental, but he really didn't care.

"Liam, please," Troy begged as his head felt as though it were ready to explode. Liam stroked harder, and Troy tumbled over the edge, coming blindingly hard on his chest.

"Troy!" Liam cried and stilled, coming deep within his body.

Once he came back to himself, Troy heard Liam breathing hard and felt him stroking his side. Pulling Liam forward, Troy kissed him deeply, loving every second he had with this man as he held him close. Liam slipped from his body, and Troy gasped softly into their kiss before helping Liam settle on the bed.

"What do I do with…?" Liam tilted his head downward, and Troy smiled.

"Go into the bathroom and remove it, then clean yourself up. I'll be right here waiting for you."

Liam got off the bed and cracked open the door, peering out before hurrying across. Troy heard the door close, and a few minutes later Liam walked back in with a towel around his waist. He was just about to close the door when they heard a knock.

"Come out to the living room when you're finished," Wally said through the door.

"Okay, thank you," Liam answered before dropping the towel and climbing onto the bed. "It looks like we're wanted."

"Yes, we are," Troy agreed as Liam snuggled close to him. Whatever they were needed for could wait a few minutes until they were done holding each other. After a while, they both dressed and wandered out into the living room, where Phillip and Haven had joined Dakota, Wally, and Jefferson. Once again, the others were talking about the mine while they drowned their worries in ice cream, and it didn't take much convincing for Liam and Troy to join in.

"I heard what sounded like a wolf cry a few days ago," Troy commented once he'd been given a huge bowl of mint chocolate chip. "Manny seemed to take exception, though."

Dakota chuckled. "Who'd have thought lions would make great wolf repellant? But they seem to. Before Manny, Wally had Schian, and he did the same thing." Dakota took a bite of what looked like cookies and cream ice cream.

"Have you had wolves around here before?" Troy asked, and he saw Dakota scowl for a second before looking over at Wally indulgently. "When we met, Wally had this thing for wolves. One of the hands shot one, and he and Phillip rescued it. I was ready to kill them both, especially since the wolf was a female."

"I know you were, but my charms won you over," Wally teased before continuing the story. "It was a mated pair, and the male mourned her loss every night," Wally added defensively. "Dakota talks tough, but he's a big softie. Anyway, once she was on the mend, I sedated her, and Dakota helped me take her back to where Phillip and I got her. We've heard them occasionally, so we're careful to keep the young cattle near the ranch, and if the cats smell them or hear them, they raise a ruckus like you heard the other night."

"Have you ever seen them, other than the one you rescued?" Troy felt a touch of excitement in his stomach and set the ice cream aside. "Have some of the other ranchers?"

"I have a few times over the last few years. It's pretty rare, but I know they're around. Mostly they stick to the park, but since they relocated the wolves in the nineties, their range has been expanding," Wally explained. "Did you know that wolves mate for life? I know they pose a danger to our cattle, that's why we take precautions, but the thing is that the parks need them, and quite frankly, so do we. The wolves keep down other predators and varmints that pose a potentially far bigger threat to our herds than the wolves. Small animals carry diseases that can cost us a lot more than wolves."

Troy saw Dakota nodding slowly as if he was agreeing under duress, and Troy settled back on the sofa, leaning slightly against Liam.

"Is there a reason for the questions?" Dakota asked as he finished his treat and set the bowl aside.

Troy didn't want to get anyone's hopes up, so he demurred slightly. "I have an idea, but I'm not sure it'll pan out. I've tried making a few calls, but haven't heard anything back. I'm going to make a few more tomorrow. If anything comes of it, I'll let you know," Troy explained, and Dakota seemed to accept his answer, but from the look on Liam's face, Troy was going to have to explain more, hopefully later. "When do you head back to the hospital?" Troy asked, trying to change the subject. He wasn't being evasive on purpose; he just didn't want to get anyone's hopes up.

"I leave tomorrow morning," Dakota answered, and Wally set down his bowl, moving until he was seated on the arm of Dakota's chair. Wally leaned against Dakota, and Troy felt Liam take his cue from them and lean closer as well. Dakota did a fake yawn that wasn't fooling anyone. "Are you ready for bed, Dad?"

"Yes," Jefferson answered. He'd been mostly asleep in his chair for a while. Wally stood up, and Dakota wheeled his father down the hallway. Wally gathered up the dishes and took them into the kitchen before saying good night as well.

"Do you really think you have some ace up your sleeve?" Haven asked, obviously skeptical.

"I don't know what we have, if anything, but could you show me where these wolves have been spotted?" Troy asked, and both Haven and Phillip nodded.

"I can show you the gully where Wally and I found the female a few years ago," Phillip offered. "I don't know if it will help."

"Wolves are territorial, so it might," Troy said.

"How do you know so much about wolves?" Haven grilled.

"Internet research," Troy answered, without adding too much about his sources.

"Haven, stop it," Phillip chastised him. "If Troy can help, let him do it his way. If he finds something, he'll tell us. Meanwhile, we continue with our other efforts." Phillip stood up and walked toward the door. "Come on, it's time for us to go. We'll see you in the morning and show you what we can." Haven said his good-nights as well and actually looked apologetic as he and Phillip left.

"I should go too," Troy told Liam. "But I'll see you first thing in the morning."

"You could stay," Liam said, leaving Troy feeling sorely tempted.

"I'd love to, but I shouldn't. I need some time to think a little, and I can't do that with your hotness right next to me." Troy saw Liam chewing his lip the way he did when he was nervous. "I don't regret anything, and I'm not having second thoughts." Troy leaned in for a kiss. "I just need to think things through a little. That's all." Troy headed for the door. "Shoot, I forgot to ask Wally if Sofia could come over tomorrow to see the animals."

"I'll take care of it in the morning, but I don't see why not," Liam said, kissing him one more time before Troy headed out into the night, where there were flashes of lightning on the horizon.

TROY regretted his decision to go back to the cabin as soon as he closed the rustic door behind him. The small rooms felt empty and vacant, and Troy was never so happy to see the sun lighten his windows in the morning. He'd wanted time to think, and he'd gotten that, since he'd barely slept at all. Checking his clock, Troy knew it was too early to call Jeanie, but he knew they'd be up and about at the ranch, so he cleaned up and dressed, eating a quick breakfast before taking the truck down the hill.

In the yard, Liam, Wally, and Phillip met him, and Liam hugged him tight as soon as he was out of the truck. "It was lonely last night," Liam whispered, and Troy told him the same.

"Did Dakota leave already?" Troy asked Wally without releasing Liam.

"Early this morning," Wally answered sadly, and Troy figured it must be hard each time he left.

"Okay, if you two are done canoodling, let's get this show on the road," Phillip teased before starting off around the back of the house. "Wally kept the wolf in the old shed over there."

"And I found her in the flood wash over here," Wally said before leading them across the range past the cat and other animal enclosures toward the far edge of the range. As they approached, Troy noticed that Wally and Phillip slowed before getting too close, peering cautiously over the edge. "She was right down there." Wally pointed the way, and Troy slipped down the damp bank to the bottom. A small amount of water ran through it from the rain the night before. Troy wasn't sure what he was expecting, other than maybe a she-wolf looking back at him, but no such luck.

"Hey, Troy," Wally called excitedly, kneeling near one edge of the culvert. "Look at this." Wally pointed to the ground. "Looks like we had a visitor here last night." Wally pointed to what looked like the track of a large dog. Troy smiled and pulled out his phone, snapping a few pictures. "Why are you interested in all this? I think it's time to be straight with us."

"I will," Troy promised, "but we need to finish up out here. Have you seen other wolves around here?"

"Over near the woods at the edge of the range. But only rarely," Wally offered somewhat reluctantly.

"Okay. Liam and I will take a look, and when we get back to the house, we'll talk," Troy said, and for a second he thought Phillip was going to argue, but Wally tapped him on the shoulder and they started back toward the house. "Let's go take a look." Troy started walking briskly across the range with Liam at his side.

"I don't understand what we're looking for," Liam said.

"I'm not sure, either. I'm working a hunch, though I'm not sure it'll pay off. But if it has any hope at all, I need some proof. We have part of it, and if we can get a little more, it would help."

"Proof of what?"

"Wolves in the area," Troy answered patiently.

"Why would we want wolves in the area? It's best if they stay away from the cattle and hunt elsewhere," Liam explained as he hurried to keep up with Troy's excitedly brisk pace.

"Maybe not in this case," Troy answered, slowing as they approached the woods. The soil was still soft from the rain the night before, and Troy walked slowly along the edge, keeping in a rough line with the tracks in the gully. Sure enough, he came on a set at the edge of the woods. They weren't very deep, and if he hadn't already seen the earlier ones, he probably wouldn't have noticed them. Troy took a number of pictures of the area as well as of the tracks. "I need you to pay close attention to where we found the tracks in case you need to back up my story."

"Okay," Liam said with resignation before looking around. "I'm ready when you are."

Together they headed back to the ranch, and Troy slipped his hand into Liam's. As they got close to the house, Troy heard yelling and then a gun blast. Both of them began running toward the sound, and as they turned the corner of the house, they saw Wally standing in front of the porch, gun in the air. Following his gaze, they saw a truck turning out of the end of the drive. "That looked like—" Liam began.

"The bastard, yeah. He started by asking where you were. Our conversation quickly degenerated to threats and ended with my gun pointed at his head." Wally's expression softened. "I thought he was going to wet himself, especially when I lowered the gun and told him I was going for his manhood first, that is, if I could find it." Wally rolled his eyes before turning to go inside the house. "Did you find what you were looking for?"

"I think so." Troy's phone rang, and he fished it out of his pocket. "It's Jeanie." Troy answered it and asked her to hang on a second. "Is it okay if she and Sofia come over to see the horses?"

Liam looked at Wally, who nodded. "As long as everyone behaves," Wally answered sarcastically before continuing inside. Troy took the call and made arrangements before hanging up. "She got a rental car and said she and Sofia would be out in about an hour. I know you're nervous, but she's basically a nice person, you'll see."

"Do you think Sofia will like me?" There was that nervous chewing on his lower lip again.

"Take her on her first real ride on a horse and she'll be your friend for life, I promise." Troy smiled and motioned for Liam to go first; he had some phone calls to make and some explaining to do.

Chapter Nine

LIAM was extremely nervous, and Troy was being rather mysterious, even if he seemed as excited as a kid. Liam was more than curious about what Troy had in mind, but there were chores to get done and the cats hadn't been fed yet that morning. Liam got the food and met some growly cats, who immediately pounced on their meat as though they hadn't eaten in days. Liam knew he had to be careful around the large predators and tried not to think about his father's visit or the fact that Troy's ex-wife and daughter were going to be here anytime. His mind wandered anyway, and Liam jumped back when Shahrazad snarled at him. "Oh, give it up, you grumpy old thing. No one is going to take your breakfast," Liam snarled back, and the cat lifted her head away from the food for a second, tilting it as though she were intrigued before returning to her meal.

When Liam was done, he put everything away before heading to the barn. There were plenty of chores to get done, and he needed to keep busy. Before going into the barn, he saw Troy sitting on the porch, talking on the phone. Wandering over, Liam heard him speaking earnestly. "I have proof, witnesses as well as photographs. I'll text them to you as soon as we hang up. And I've even heard them myself." Troy got quiet for a few seconds as he listened, and then motioned Liam over, but Liam pointed to the barn, and Troy nodded. "I'll see if I can get more, but they're definitely here, and this is part of their territory now." Liam had no idea what Troy could be talking about, other than the wolves, and he went into the barn and began cleaning out one of the stalls.

"Hey, do you need some help?" Troy asked as Liam carried the last of the mulch out of the stall.

"I'm almost done," Liam explained. "But if you want to sweep the stall floor, that would be great. Then I can spread the new bedding." Liam upended the wheelbarrow, emptying the contents onto the mulch pile. "Was your call successful?"

"Sort of, I guess," Troy answered.

"Are you going to tell me about it?" Liam asked as they walked to the now empty stall, and Troy grabbed the broom and began sweeping out the last of the muck, the scent of ammonia heavy in the air.

"I'm not sure it's going to work, but I'll tell you what I'm thinking. As Dakota said, the federal government released wolves into Yellowstone in the nineties to reintroduce the species, and they've done very well. They're also protected under the Endangered Species Act. I know this is a bit complicated, but I think I've found an angle to make this work."

"How?" Liam heard Wally's voice from outside the stall.

"Yeah, how?" Mario asked from the stall doorway, his arms folded over his chest.

Troy set the broom aside and stepped out into the walkway, and everyone stopped to listen. "The mining company has leased the land, and they need water. Since they're trying to lease the water rights from the town rather than pursuing new rights, they don't need an environmental-impact study, which is one of the things they're trying to avoid because those can take years and cost a lot of money." Troy stopped and looked at each of them.

"So? We already know that," Mario said.

"And what does that have to do with the wolves?" Wally asked right behind him.

"It's complicated and bureaucratic, but if the wolves have made this area part of their territory, being that they're an endangered species and any change in the environment could affect them, the mining company would need an environmental-impact study plus possibly others to prove that taking the water will not affect the wolves." Troy smiled as though he'd made a grand pronouncement. "The mine and their water project could not proceed at all until that's done. It may not stop them right away, but it could delay them, and it would get a bunch of environmental groups on your side. The combined pressure could make the project too expensive, and it could be enough to get the town council to realize it isn't worth it, especially since they probably don't want to get drawn into any fight."

"So how does this work?" Wally asked, and Liam thought he looked somewhat impressed.

"Actually, I got the ball rolling this morning. Before I moved here, I worked for the Department of the Interior in Washington. I talked to one of my former colleagues and sent him the pictures we took. He's going to look into it to see if they've received other reports of wolves in this area to corroborate what I've told him. If he does, then that could be enough for him to order the study. We'll have to wait, but he said he'd call me and let me know."

"Is there anything we can do?" Wally asked.

"Sure. Write down when you've seen wolves on the ranch and how often. Ask the other ranchers to do the same. All we need to do is show a regular pattern of habitation to demonstrate that this is part of their territory. The more evidence we have, the easier it's going to be," Troy explained with a smile, and Liam couldn't help smiling in return.

Mario simply shook his head, an expression of disbelief coloring his face. "Who'd have thought that wolves would actually benefit us? The other ranchers are not going to believe this, that our water rights are being protected by wolves."

"Stranger things have happened," Wally commented, "but I can't think of any." Wally looked around the barn, and Liam got back to work as Wally headed to his small clinic at the back of the barn. Wally didn't do a lot of work with small animals, so he'd explained to Liam that the clinic was mostly a place to safely store his supplies. Liam finished spreading the bedding as Wally hurried out of the clinic and got into his truck, heading out on what looked like a call.

Closing the stall door, Liam looked for Troy and saw him standing near the barn door. He was about to start cleaning another stall when he heard a vehicle on the gravel out front, followed by the cries of the dogs barking like an excited greeting party. After washing his hands, Liam nervously walked toward Troy, who was shooing the dogs back.

He saw a woman get out of the car before opening the back door, and a young girl climbed out. Liam knew that it was Jeanie and Sofia, and he watched as Jeanie approached Troy with a slight smile, while Sofia looked around, wide-eyed, but made no move toward Troy. That nearly broke Liam's heart, and when Troy turned to look at him, Liam saw the hurt on his face. "Jeanie and Sofia, this is Liam," Troy said, and Jeanie walked right up to him, shaking his hand as they exchanged greetings. Sofia stayed close to her mother, and other than a soft "hello" said nothing.

"Your dad told me that you'd like to see the horses," Liam said as he knelt down to Sofia's eye level. "Would you like to ride one?" She looked adorable in pigtails, a pair of tiny jeans, and a T-shirt.

Sofia looked up at her mother, and Jeanie nodded. "Would you like that?"

Sofia nodded, and Liam saw excitement in her eyes. "Come on, then. You can meet the horse first, and then we'll get ready to go for a ride," Liam said happily, and Sofia looked at her mother before allowing Liam to take her hand and lead her into the barn. "This is Rose," Liam explained as he approached one of the older horses. "We don't ride her much because she's getting old, but I bet she'd love to give you a ride," Liam told her before lifting her up so she could look into the stall. Sofia felt light in his arms, and she giggled when Rose breathed on her.

"Horsey breath," she said with more laughter.

"Would you like to give her a treat?" Liam asked before carefully putting Sofia down and grabbing a carrot from the treat container. He handed it to Sofia before lifting her up again. "Hold it flat in your hand, and she'll take it." Sofia did as she was told and giggled again as Rose took the carrot, licking Sofia's tiny hand at the same time.

"She's nice, isn't she?" Troy asked from behind them, and Liam turned and transferred Sofia to her father.

"I'll get her saddled," Liam said and hurried away to get the tack. Liam grabbed the saddle, and when he left the tack room, he saw Troy still holding Sofia.

"She's a nice horsey," she said, and Liam smiled when he saw the happy look on Troy's face.

"Yes, she is," Troy agreed. Liam didn't approach the father and daughter, and a minute later Jeanie was standing next to Liam. Neither of them talked, and Liam continued holding the saddle as it got heavier and heavier, but neither of them made a sound as Troy and Sofia talked. Finally, Jeanie noticed Liam's predicament and tilted her head back toward the room. Liam backed up and stepped inside, putting down the saddle, and Jeanie joined him. Liam didn't know what to say, so he tried to busy himself straightening the tack and saddles.

"It's okay," Jeanie said softly. "I'm not sure how comfortable I am with this either."

Liam stopped his busy work and turned around. "I guess I expected you to have two heads or something," Liam said, not really knowing what to say. "Sofia seems adorable," he added quickly, realizing how his first statement sounded.

Thankfully, Jeanie smiled. "I know how you feel. I don't know what I expected, but it wasn't someone so young or so open." Jeanie smiled slightly. "And yes, Sofia is a dear, but she's been unhappy for months, and I know it's because she missed her daddy." Childish laughter drifted into the room, followed by deeper, more mature chuckles, and Jeanie's smile widened. "It's good to hear that again from both of them."

"You still care for him?" Liam asked, unsure why he was asking, but needing to know anyway.

"Yes, but not in the way I once did," she said as they heard more laughter and talking. "I think we can be friends now, and we need to be for Sofia's sake. She deserves two parents who love her."

"I know Troy does. Being away from her has been very hard on him," Liam said with a sigh, still not convinced that Troy wouldn't leave and go back east for the chance to be with his daughter. Liam couldn't blame him, although he knew it would break his heart.

Small, rapid footsteps outside the door broke up their conversation. "Can I go riding now?" Sofia asked before stepping into the room, looking up at Liam.

"Of course. Do you want to watch me saddle her?" Liam asked, and Sofia nodded. Liam grabbed her bit, and Sofia followed him to the stall. Liam inserted it into the horse's mouth before leading Rose out of the barn. "Daddy needs to hold the reins. I'll get the saddle, and you can watch." Liam handed the reins to Troy and retrieved the saddle and blanket. It didn't take long before Liam had Rose saddled and ready. Taking the reins from Troy, Liam let him lift his daughter up, placing her in the saddle. "Hang onto her mane. It won't hurt her," Liam said before slowly leading Rose around the yard. Sofia whooped and laughed, occasionally telling Rose she was a good horsey.

At some point, Wally's truck pulled into the drive, and Troy made introductions while Liam continued leading Sofia and Rose around the yard. "Are you ready to get down?" Jeanie asked after almost an hour, and Sofia shook her head, pigtails flying like blond whips. "If you wear Rose out, she'll be too tired for you to ride later."

Sofia gave in to superior mama logic, and Troy lifted her off. Liam led Rose back into the barn, taking off the saddle and bit before praising her profusely as he put Rose in her stall.

"Would you like to see the other animals?" Liam asked as he rejoined the others in the yard. Sofia nodded her answer vigorously.

"Okay, but you need to let Daddy carry you." Liam led them around the house and out toward the pens. He heard both Jeanie and Sofia gasp when they saw the cats.

"What are these doing here?" Jeanie asked, staying well away from the pens.

"Wally is a vet, and he runs a large animal rescue," Liam explained. "It's part of my job to feed and water the beasts." Liam moved closer to the lion's enclosure. "This is Manny. Would you say hello?" The cat stretched and yawned, licking his lips before giving them one of those bored looks that only cats can. Then he turned around and walked to the far side of the enclosure before lying down again. "He's a lion, and this is Shahrazad. She's a tiger."

She snarled and yipped fiercely, and Sofia squeaked at the sound, turning away to bury her face in Troy's shoulder. Manny took the opportunity to assert his manhood and roared his response before lying back in his spot in the sun. "Will he do that again?" Sofia asked.

"Nope, he's done," Troy explained, and they stepped back.

"What are those over there?" Sofia pointed to the other set of cages farther back.

"They're empty for now," Liam explained. Wally had said that he might be getting more animals soon. He never really knew. "Let's go back to the house." They began walking back across the range.

"Are there more animals?"

"Just the dogs and the cattle. The dogs will play with you if you want, but the cattle aren't much fun." Liam winked at Sofia, and she giggled as Troy carried her back to the house. "Would you like to come inside?" Liam asked, feeling more comfortable with Jeanie and Sofia once he let go of that fact that Jeanie was Troy's ex-wife and treated her like anyone else.

Liam held the door and let everyone else go in front of him. One of the small dogs, Benjamin, snuck inside, jumping around Sofia's legs, and she sat on the floor as the small beagle mix crawled all over her, soaking up the attention as he smothered her in doggie kisses.

"Lunch will be ready in half an hour," Wally said from the kitchen before poking his head around the corner, "I hope you and Sofia can stay," he added with a smile before returning to the kitchen. The adults sat down in the living room while Sofia played with Benjamin on the floor, having a ball.

"So, Liam, is that a Texas accent I hear?" Jeanie asked.

"Yes. I grew up on a ranch in west Texas with my father." Because of Sofia, Liam had to stop himself from saying "the bastard" in reference to his father. "My mother left when I was about ten."

"You didn't have a mommy?" Sofia asked from the floor.

Liam turned to Sofia. "Not after I was ten," he answered with much more lightness than he felt. Liam had gotten over her leaving, but the guilt his father heaped on him had left a lasting effect. "It's okay now, though," Liam added when he saw the scared look on Sofia's face. Sofia looked at her mother for a few moments until Benjamin captured her attention again, and she went back to playing.

Liam felt a slight touch on his hand as Troy lightly comforted him, letting him know he wasn't alone. Liam did not allow himself to look over at Troy because he knew his emotions would get the best of him. He was sitting here with Jeanie and Sofia, and Troy was comforting *him*. Troy smiled at him once Liam chanced a glance before turning back to Jeanie.

"What do you do, Jeanie?"

"I'm an interior decorator. When Troy and I were together, I worked part time, but lately I've been working more. I really like it." Jeanie sounded excited, and Liam could tell what she said was true.

"What do you do with Sofia?" Liam asked, because he could almost read the question on Troy's face.

"She comes with me sometimes. Most of what I do is on the phone or scouting around town for the right item. Sofia's a great little shopper, so we often go together." Jeanie looked happy; Liam could see it, and he thought Troy could see it as well.

Wally joined them for a little while until his timer went off in the kitchen. Then he got up again, and a few minutes later called everyone to lunch.

The table was a little crowded, especially when Wally wheeled Jefferson to the table. Sofia kept looking at him all through dinner. "Did you hurt yourself?" she finally asked, her curiosity getting the best of her.

"Nah," Jefferson answered. "I just got old and cranky." He winked at her, and Sofia slid off her seat and stood near Jefferson, watching him closely.

"What happened to your legs?"

"Sofia," her mother cut in. "That's not a nice question to ask."

"They stopped working a while ago. But now I have wheels. If you clean your plate, I'll give you a ride." Jefferson smiled, and Sofia hurried back to her place. The conversation around the table sounded a lot like what Liam thought a regular family would sound like.

"Did you hear anything from your contact?" Wally asked.

"Not yet. Have you had any luck?"

"Yup." Wally grinned. "Milford, up the way, has seen wolves and has been tracking them on his property for a while. He said he wanted to use the data to make a case for getting rid of them. He's going to send it over later today, and you can forward it on." Wally filled everyone in on the situation.

"You know," Jeanie said as she sat back from her plate, smiling, "if this is ranch food, I may move out here."

Wally began to laugh hard. "Yeah, you could specialize in decorating with wagon-wheel coffee tables." Jeanie made a face, and everyone roared, including her. Once lunch was done, Liam helped clean up. One of the highlights of the afternoon was Sofia sitting on Jefferson's lap as Wally wheeled them both around the house.

The phone rang, and Liam answered it since he was closest.

"May I speak with Liam please?"

"This is he," Liam answered, not recognizing the voice right away.

"This is John Fabian."

"Oh, yes, the lawyer," Liam said, remembering their conversation from a few days ago.

"Can you talk? I suggest you go somewhere private," he said, and Liam felt a knot forming in his stomach. The wonderful lunch they'd just had suddenly wasn't sitting so well.

"Just a minute," Liam answered and covered the phone with his hand. "Can I use Dakota's office?" Liam asked Wally, who walked to where Liam was standing.

"Of course. Is everything okay?" The concern in Wally's voice must have caught Troy's attention because he joined them.

"I don't know; it's the lawyer," Liam answered.

"Of course. Go ahead and use the office. I'll hang up the phone here when you're ready," Wally said, taking the receiver. Liam walked down the hallway and entered the empty office, closing the door behind him. Picking up the phone, he told Wally he had it and heard the extension click as it hung up.

"I'm here," Liam said.

"Then I'll get right down to business. I was able to do more research, and it's as I thought. I've been in touch with a colleague I know from law school. He's a lawyer in Texas and he was very helpful. It hasn't been easy to unravel everything, but I think between the two of us, we've been able to do it." Liam heard a soft knock and then the door opened. Troy's face poked through the opening, and Liam motioned him inside as he listened to the lawyer explain everything. Troy stood next to him, and

Liam felt his strong hands on his shoulder, massaging him lightly as the lawyer continued explaining things. Liam understood only part of what he said, but what he did understand tore away the last shred of positive emotion he had for his father. "Liam, is that what you want to do?"

"Yes," he answered blankly, barely able to listen to what he was being told. "Do it all." Liam felt Troy's hand on his arm, comforting him as he began to shake with hurt and anger. "I want him out of my life."

"Okay. I'll get the ball rolling on this end. You do what you need to, and make sure you aren't alone," the lawyer cautioned, and Liam agreed. "I'll call you when I have an update, and you'll need to come in to sign all the papers."

"I will," Liam answered before numbly placing the phone in the cradle.

"I take it you didn't get good news," Troy said softly, and Liam shook his head.

"I guess it depends on how you look at it," Liam answered. "I need to make one phone call, and then I'm done." Liam picked up the phone and dialed the cell number he knew by heart. "Dad, it's Liam."

"Have you signed the papers?" his father asked in a rush, getting right to what he wanted.

"I'll have them for you. Be at the ranch at six o'clock tonight and you can pick them up. I don't want to see you before then, and afterwards, I never want to see your sorry ass ever again. And that means around town, and it most certainly means no late-night visits to the ranch." Liam didn't give his father a chance to answer. "I'll see you at six and that will be the last time I ever see you." Liam hung up the phone and gasped a deep breath, closing his eyes to stop the tears that threatened. *Damn it, I will not cry over that bastard. No way.*

"You going to be okay?" Troy whispered, hugging Liam close. "I know that was hard. He may have been a bastard, but he was still your father and you have every right to grieve the loss." Liam placed his head on Troy's shoulder and said nothing, simply letting himself be held for a while.

"I'm going to be fine," Liam finally answered, stepping away from Troy's warmth and immediately missing it. "We need to get back to Jeanie and Sofia."

"They'll keep a few minutes. Sofia and Jefferson are having a ball together. Last I looked, they were watching baseball, and he was explaining things to her," Troy said as Liam was once again held tight. "Right now, I'm more worried about you and what's happening with your father."

Liam held his breath. "I'll tell you all about it, but I need a few minutes to get my head around it. Besides, I need to talk to Wally as well."

"I heard you tell him to come here at six," Troy said.

"Yes. And the lawyer is arranging for him to get an interesting reception. So let's join your family, and once they leave, we'll sit down and I'll tell you everything." Troy didn't look completely convinced. "Trust me. This could prove to be quite entertaining."

"I do trust you. I didn't mean to imply otherwise. I'm just concerned about what the bastard is putting you through," Troy whispered in Liam's ear, and Liam shivered, regardless of the message he was delivering. Liam loved being this close to Troy. He felt safe in his arms and he never wanted to leave this room, but they had people visiting and plenty of things to get ready.

"Go spend time with your daughter," Liam said with a soft sigh as Troy nipped at his ear.

"Don't think I haven't noticed what you've been doing as far as Sofia is concerned," Troy said softly. "I love you for it."

Liam turned in his arms. "She's your daughter. The two of you needed to have fun together."

"Well, we have, and that's mostly due to you." Troy nipped lightly at the base of Liam's neck before the hug slipped away. Troy opened the door just as Sofia raced by with Benjamin right on her heels, the dog barking and Sofia laughing. Troy gave Liam another "grateful father" look before leaving the office.

Liam closed the door and sank into one of the chairs, mulling over everything the lawyer had told him and silently contemplating what he wanted to do. Looking around the desk, Liam found a phone book and began thumbing through the very front, stopping at the page he wanted before staring at the number. Once he did this, there would be no turning back. He remained where he was until Wally opened the door and peered inside. "Everything okay?"

Liam didn't move and he felt Wally walk inside and close the door.

"I'm trying to decide what to do," Liam said, still staring at the phone number. "Once I do this, I can't change it." Liam looked up and saw Wally looking at the entry in the phone book as well.

"Don't do it for revenge, but because it's the right thing to do," was Wally's advice. No matter what, though, Liam knew this, more than anything else, had to be his decision. Liam looked into Wally's face, seeing his encouraging smile. Holding his breath, Liam picked up the phone and began to dial.

THE rest of the afternoon was pleasant enough. Liam was on edge for much of it, but kept his mind on his work and off what was to come. Sofia asked for another ride on Rose, so Liam saddled her and let Troy lead her around the yard while he got his chores done. It was good to hear her laugh, and whenever he emptied a load of muck from the stalls, he saw the smile on Troy's face, and that was worth going through whatever life sent his way. After cleaning the stalls, Liam wandered out to the enclosures to check on the cats and make sure they had water. As he was finishing, he heard footsteps behind him. He expected to see Wally, but was surprised when Jeanie approached cautiously.

"Are they okay?" she asked, stopping a good distance from the fencing.

"They're fine. It's warm, so they'll spend most of the afternoon doing as little as possible," Liam explained as he finished filling Manny's water.

"Troy loves you," Jeanie said with a bit of hurt in her voice. "I won't lie to you and say that I hadn't hoped he'd have changed."

"You came to get him back?" Liam asked.

Jeanie shrugged a little sadly. "I don't think so, but I wouldn't have minded if he'd have asked. I guess it would have validated that there wasn't something wrong with me."

"There isn't," Liam said as he began rolling up the hose. "There isn't anything wrong with him, either. He is the way he is. I'm sorry he lied to you, but he was lying to himself as well, and it ate away at him. He's started to get past the guilt and shame he's carried around for so long. I think we both have."

"You really love him, don't you?" Jeanie asked, and then she put up her hand. "You don't have to answer that, because I can see it in your eyes when you look at him. And in his when he looks at you. He's happy in a way I haven't seen him in quite a while."

"I guess the question is, are you happy too?" Liam asked as he turned off the water at the spigot and then rolled up the hose, setting it near the house.

"Not completely, but I will be. When I married Troy, I thought it was forever, and I found out it wasn't."

"If it's any consolation, I think he felt the same way. His feelings hurt him as much as they hurt you, maybe more, because he didn't want to feel them."

Jeanie smiled. "You know, for someone so young, you're pretty smart."

Liam wasn't sure how to respond, but the compliment pleased him, and he watched her walk around the house, presumably to where Sofia was still getting her horsey ride.

"Liam," Wally called from the back door. "Do you think you can get the enclosures in the other bay ready by tomorrow afternoon?" Liam looked at the empty area and nodded. There wasn't a lot to do. "The state animal control called. They found four lions in a house in Cheyenne that someone decided to try to keep as pets. They're still cubs, and they said they're undernourished and not in the best shape. They're bringing them by tomorrow."

"No problem," Liam answered.

"Thank you," Wally said before closing the door. Liam walked around to the front of the house and saw Troy helping Sofia off Rose's back. Liam watched as Sofia put her arms around his neck. He would have loved to hear what she said, but the sheer joy on Troy's face as he hugged his daughter tight told him plenty. Liam waited until Troy had set Sofia down before approaching.

"I'm going to take Sofia back to town," Jeanie explained. "We'll be back tomorrow and we'll bring her suitcase. She can stay with you for a few days, and then we need to fly home."

"What are you going to do?" Troy asked Jeanie, as Liam took Rose's reins.

Liam heard Jeanie's laugh as he walked Rosie toward the barn. "Probably spend two whole days in bed and not do a thing except read and lay by the pool."

The rest of the conversation was lost, but Liam didn't mind. Troy was happy, and that was what mattered. For the second time that day, Liam unsaddled Rose, and this time he put her in one of the empty paddocks to graze. She'd earned it. When he came back out, it was just in time to wave good-bye to Jeanie and Sofia as they pulled out of the yard and started down the drive. The calm that had overtaken Liam was almost immediately replaced by apprehension over what he was about to do.

"You don't have to do this," Troy said as he moved closer. "This could be handled by Wally and me without you being there."

"No, it can't. I have to do this just so I can stop wondering and feeling cowardly for the rest of my life," Liam explained. "I have to stand up to him face to face, man to man. I feel like that's the only way I'll ever be able to be rid of him."

"Okay, but Wally and I will be there. You don't have to do this alone. Not anymore," Troy told him. Liam knew that was true. Both Troy and Wally had already backed him up more often in the weeks he'd known them than his father ever had in all the years Liam could remember. "Go get cleaned up, and I'll wait out here."

Liam nodded and walked inside, going straight to the room he was using and grabbing some fresh clothes before heading to the bathroom. Liam tried to relax and let his anxiety go away, but it wouldn't, and he knew nothing would change until this was over.

Stepping beneath the shower spray, Liam closed his eyes and pushed away everything but Troy. Images of his lover flashed through his mind as Liam washed himself. He hadn't known him long, but Troy had become as essential to him as air. Running his hands over his skin, Liam let his mind center on Troy, and he found as long as he did that, the jitters receded and he was able to think. Liam finished washing and stepped under the water to rinse, wondering if he could convince Troy this evening that they both needed another one of these. There were so many fantasies he wanted to try, and sex in the shower was moving up on his list. First things first, though. Liam turned off the water and dried himself before dressing in his best clothes. Checking the time, Liam realized it was nearly six, and he headed outside.

Liam couldn't see Troy and Wally, but he knew they were around, and Liam tensed when he saw his father's truck turn into the drive and pull to a stop near the house.

"So, you said you have the signed papers," his father began almost before he was out of the vehicle.

"Actually, I have signed the papers, but they aren't here. They're with my lawyer, and a copy of them is with the lawyer in Texas." Liam stood his ground even as his father walked closer.

"I need those papers signed so I can sell the ranch!"

"You mean *my* ranch. Yes, I know about the trust and the restrictions, and I am selling the ranch, but you aren't getting any of it."

The bastard laughed. "I'm the trustee, and you can't do anything about it until you're twenty-five." Then his father's laughter died away, and his eyes blazed.

"Actually, that's not true. You see, my lawyer in Texas has gotten you removed as trustee, and a neutral party has been appointed. The ranch is going to be sold, and you're being evicted. Your things are being moved out as we speak. I don't know what my lawyer is doing with them, but I hope he's making a huge bonfire. Because there's nothing there for you anymore at all. You've hurt me and taken from me for the last time, you total bastard!"

Liam didn't even see the fist until it was on the way to his chin. Liam whirled around and fell to the ground, tasting blood and feeling as though his head had been rattled.

"You little shit. I will bury you right here. That ranch is mine!"

"Did you open the gates here?"

"Of course I did! Damned faggots! Put a good scare into you, didn't I? Now, come on. You're coming back with me and getting all this called off." His father reached for him, but Liam moved out of his reach and got to his feet, staring at his father.

"No, that's not going to happen. I've had it with you, and you've used me as a punching bag and whipping boy for the last time."

"I can agree with that," a rough, strong voice said from the barn. "Don't touch that man again! Now get on the ground!"

Liam was afraid to turn, watching his father turn pale and step back. Then Liam glanced toward the voice and saw the sheriff with his gun drawn, pointed at his father, one of his deputies standing next to him, his hand on his weapon. The sheriff came closer, and Liam moved toward where Troy stood and felt his lover's arms wrap around him.

"Young man, you should never have put yourself in danger, but you gave us plenty to work with." The sheriff cuffed his father, leaving him on the ground. "We take cattle rustling very seriously here," the sheriff told his father. "And I also have a warrant from the state of Texas. It seems they want to talk to you about attempts to defraud your son's trust."

The deputy holstered his weapon before bringing around a large sedan from the side yard. It wasn't marked, but as soon as the door opened, it was immediately apparent it was a sheriff's vehicle. The deputy got his father inside as he began spouting vitriol and anger at all of them. He began to fight the deputy. "You continue to struggle, and I will taze you into the middle of next week!"

His father stopped struggling, but the steady stream of obscenities continued until the door closed. Even through the windows, Liam could see his father continuing his tirade.

"That man's a piece of work, but I have a cell he can cool off in until Texas decides what they want to do with him," the sheriff said before turning to Liam. "Are you all right? We can get an ambulance if you need one."

"No," Liam said, flexing his jaw. "He's done much worse over the years. I'll be fine."

"We'll all be down tomorrow to give you our statements," Wally said. "We need to make sure he's gone for good."

"He will be, Wally. Don't worry about that." The sheriff shook all their hands before getting into his car. "We'll see y'all tomorrow at the station." With a satisfied smile, the sheriff and his deputy headed down the drive.

"I think that's enough excitement for quite a while." Wally looked at Troy. "I take it you're staying for dinner," Wally said warmly.

"If that's okay," Liam said.

"Of course, but it's Troy's turn to cook," Wally said with a wink and a smile before turning toward the front door.

"Come on," Troy told him, taking his hand. "Let's get you cleaned up and your lip looked at."

"I'm okay," Liam insisted. He was fine, actually, more than fine. He'd looked his abusive father in the eye and stood up to the old bastard. "I feel like I've exorcised the demon, you know?" Liam smiled and then winced at the pain in his split lip.

"I guess, in a way, I do too." Troy smiled back and took Liam's hand as they went into the house. Troy led him right through to the bathroom and got a cloth. After wetting it, Troy gently washed the blood off his lover's face. "This is probably going to sting, but hold still so I can get it all."

"Ow," Liam said, and he jumped when the cloth hit the cut on his swollen lip. Liam steadied himself as Troy continued cleaning him up. "Are you really going to stay?" Liam figured it was better to ask and know for sure than to keep guessing.

Troy stopped moving his hand and lowered it away from Liam's skin. "Yes, I'm really going to stay. I like it here." Troy finished washing Liam's lip before rinsing the cloth and hanging it to dry.

"I wouldn't blame you if you wanted to live closer to Sofia," Liam said, lowering his gaze to the counter, and after a few seconds, he felt fingers lifting his chin.

"Sofia will come here to visit, and *we'll* visit them there as well."

"We?" Liam asked hopefully, a smile sending a stab of pain through his lip, but he didn't really care.

"Yes, we." Troy's eyes looked serious as he curled his mouth into a smile. "Jeanie and I need to figure out the details, but I believe we can work it out. And I'm sure Sofia won't need much convincing, especially if there are horsey rides involved." Troy moved closer, and Liam felt Troy's warmth as his eyes drifted closed. Light, cautious kisses touched his lips, and Liam responded carefully. "I love you," Troy said softly, and Liam felt his warm breath on his tingling lips.

"I love you too," Liam echoed before kissing Troy more strongly this time, heedless of the pain in his lips.

A forceful knock made both of them jump. "If you're doing anything in there, you need to finish up. Dinner is ready." Wally sounded amused, and Liam sighed before moving away from Troy's warmth and opening the door. The scent of food filled the house, and Liam followed his nose, with Troy right behind him.

"Since you were busy, I took care of dinner, but it's still your turn," Wally said with a wink as he opened the oven door and took out the casserole dish. It looked like leftovers, but Liam didn't mind, and he figured Troy didn't, either.

"We need to go fishing again," Troy said as he pulled out a chair. "Since I have Sofia tomorrow, how about I take you all to the steakhouse for dinner?"

"Deal," Wally said as he placed the dish in the middle of the table before wheeling Jefferson to the table. They chattered and ate, with Liam as excited and relieved as he could ever remember being. There would be no more beatings and fights, no more of the put-downs and name-calling that had ripped his self-image to shreds over the years. The abuse was over. Troy lightly touched his leg beneath the table, and Liam looked at him, smiling.

"You didn't hear anything?" Wally inquired.

"No," Troy answered. "Sometimes these things take time. I'll fax over the information from Mr. Milford after dinner. If we don't hear in a week, I'll call again. It's a bureaucracy that moves at its own pace, and unfortunately there are times when it can seem glacial."

Liam saw Wally nod, and they continued eating, talking about other things. At the end of the meal, he and Troy cleaned up, and then Liam went out back to check that the cats were okay for the night. "Where's Wally?" Liam asked when he saw Troy walk out of the barn, looking at him intensely before striding over to him and kissing him hard.

"You know," Troy began when he broke the kiss, "I've always had this barn-sex fantasy."

Liam chuckled. "You know that hay is really scratchy, especially on the tender parts?" Liam lightly returned Troy's kiss. "I've always had this shower fantasy and—" Troy cut him off with a kiss, and then they headed toward the house. Hopefully, they had enough time for all their fantasies.

Epilogue

"SO YOU'RE really staying there permanently," Kevin said, and Troy laughed. "You know they get snow by the foot and freeze-your-ass temperatures."

"Tell me about it. Last night was below freezing. I woke up to three inches of snow on the ground, and it's only November. But I have Liam to keep me warm." Liam had done much more than just keep him warm last night, but Troy kept that to himself.

"I'll bet you do," Kevin quipped. "It sounds like you're happy, and that's good to hear. It's been a while." Kevin chuckled lightly. "There's another reason I called. I was wondering if you'd made a decision about what you wanted to do with the hunting cabin."

"I think so. I asked Liam if he'd like to get a place together, and he was extremely enthusiastic, to say the least." The memory of just how enthusiastic made Troy squirm just a little, and he was more than glad Kevin couldn't see him right now. "I think it's best we sell it, but I want to be careful about who we sell it to."

"Okay. You handle it on that end. I'll trust your judgment." That statement nearly blew Troy away. He and Kevin hadn't had a trusting relationship in a long time. Troy tried not to feel guilty and instead kept his attention on the discussion. "Let me know when you have something."

"I will," Troy promised, and they talked for a while longer before ending the call. Placing his phone in his pocket, Troy looked around the now empty and darkening cabin and grabbed the last box of his things, making a final trip to his truck. Wally had given him a place to store his stuff until he and Liam decided what they wanted to do. Wally had also explained that the snow could start at any time, and once it did, he probably wouldn't be able to get back up to the cabin until spring.

Placing the last box with the others, Troy shut and locked the cabin door before walking to his truck and driving down the hill and over to the ranch.

"Is this the last of it?" Liam asked excitedly as soon as Troy opened his door.

"Yes."

"Good. I think I found us a place to live. It's a small house on this side of town. It's not too far from the ranch, and we can stop mooching off Wally and Dakota." Liam was so excited Troy wondered if he was going to burst. He knew that having his very own place to live was a big thing for Liam, sort of a place of his own.

"It sounds perfect. Can we look at it together tomorrow?" Troy found Liam's excitement contagious, and he got out of the truck, hugging his lover tight. "Where is everyone?"

"At the town hall, remember? It's the meeting when the council is supposed to make a final decision on the water rights. It's taken them months and nearly divided the town, but tonight they're supposed to announce a decision," Liam said with a smile.

"We'll see. The mining companies can be tenacious, especially when they think they can make money," Troy explained and then gave Liam a kiss before releasing him and turning to begin unloading the last of the boxes. It didn't take long, and Troy helped Liam with evening chores before they went inside.

The phone rang as they walked in, and Liam answered it. "Well, that was fast," Troy heard him say. "Then we'll see you soon." Troy heard Liam hang up. "They're on their way back, and Wally sounded happy. He said he'd tell us everything when he and Dakota get home."

It wasn't long before footsteps on the porch announced their arrival, and the door opened with Dakota, Wally, Haven, and Phillip walking in, each with a huge smile on his face. "They turned them down," Dakota said happily. "I need to tell Dad. Wally, open a bottle of something. We need to celebrate."

Dakota's footsteps softened as he walked down the hallway, and Wally strode into the kitchen, returning with a bottle of what looked like Champagne. Once Dakota returned, Wally popped the cork. Liam got glasses, and Wally poured and passed them around. "To Troy," Dakota said as he lifted his glass, "for making Washington work for us."

"I take it the environmental-impact study knocked the fight out of the mining company," Troy said after sipping from his glass.

"Sort of," Dakota said. "I talked to one of the council members, and he said they were just waiting for them to make good on their pledge to the community center before turning them down. Getting Washington involved gave them cover to do what they wanted to do. Most people weren't happy about the mining company, but council couldn't justify saying no to the jobs. They could now, and did. Small-town politics will drive you crazy."

Troy smiled. "I'm glad I could help."

"You did more than help. You were the key to the whole thing," Dakota told him, and Troy peeked at Liam, who smiled at him. Dakota sat in one of the chairs before setting his glass on the coffee table. "Wally said on the way back that you have something you want to discuss with us."

Troy nodded and sat next to Liam, holding his hand. "My brother and I have decided to sell the cabin and the land. What I wanted to know is if you'd like to add the land, and more importantly, access to the stream, to the ranch. It would give you a second source of water," Troy explained, and he felt Liam nudge his side. "You don't need to decide anything until spring."

Dakota smiled and looked at Wally and Haven, nodding slowly. "We've thought you might want to sell, and yes, we'd be very interested in the land. I'm sure we can work out the details, but this incident has taught all of us that we need a second source of water." Dakota lifted his glass and clinked it on Troy's.

The evening's celebration continued until Phillip and Haven headed home, and then Liam gave Troy his "time for bed" look, and they said good night as well.

Liam moved close in the cool room, that had become theirs over the past few months, sliding his hands beneath Troy's shirt. "I love you, Troy," Liam said with a sad smile.

"What's that for?" Troy asked.

"It's going to be hard to move away from here. This was the first place I really felt accepted and welcomed."

"I know. This place is very special for me too. Mostly because it's where I found you," Troy said, nearly touching his lips to Liam's.

"We found each other," Liam corrected before kissing him. "We both were trying to get away from our lives, and in the process...."

"We found love," Troy added, finishing the sentence before engaging Liam's lips in something much more important than talking.

ANDREW GREY grew up in western Michigan with a father who loved to tell stories and a mother who loved to read them. Since then he has lived throughout the country and traveled throughout the world. He has a master's degree from the University of Wisconsin-Milwaukee and works in information systems for a large corporation. Andrew's hobbies include collecting antiques, gardening, and leaving his dirty dishes anywhere but in the sink (particularly when writing). He considers himself blessed with an accepting family, fantastic friends, and the world's most supportive and loving partner. Andrew currently lives in beautiful historic Carlisle, Pennsylvania.

Visit Andrew's web site at http://www.andrewgreybooks.com and blog at http://andrewgreybooks.livejournal.com/. E-mail him at andrewgrey @comcast.net.

Also by ANDREW GREY

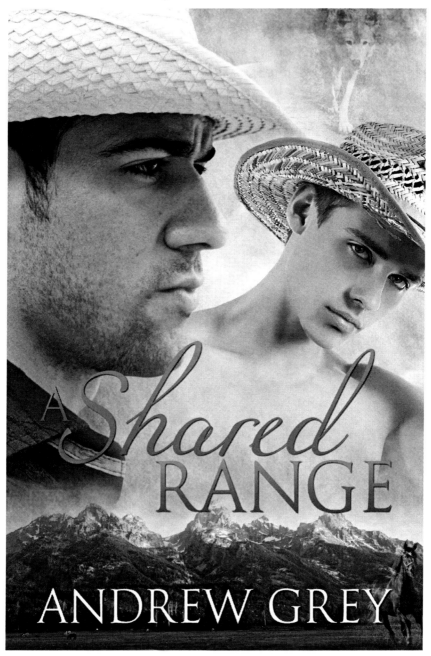

A Shared RANGE

ANDREW GREY

http://www.dreamspinnerpress.com

A TROUBLED Range

ANDREW GREY

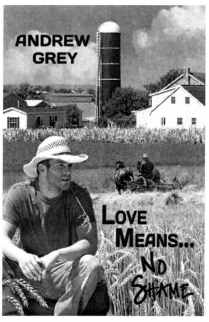

http://www.dreamspinnerpress.com

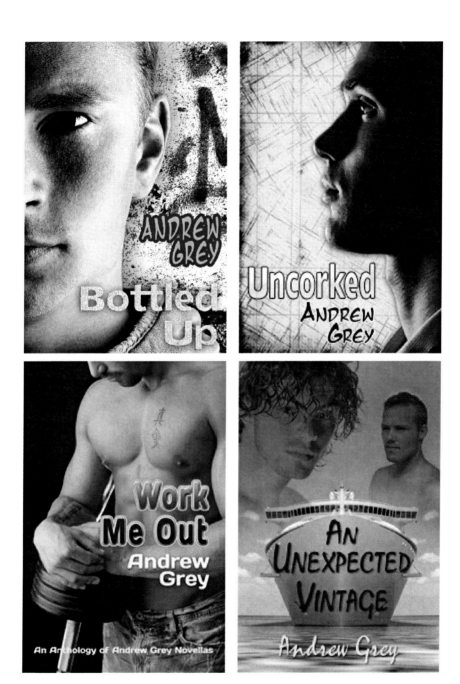

http://www.dreamspinnerpress.com

http://www.dreamspinnerpress.com

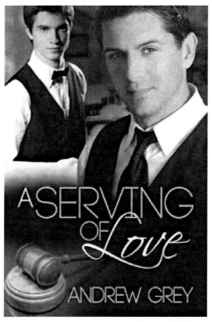

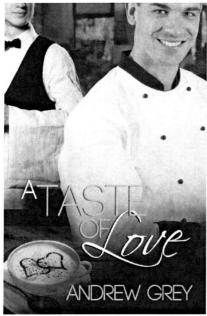

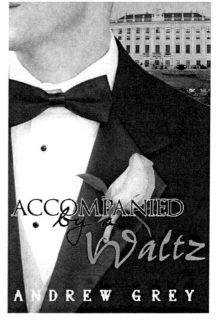

http://www.dreamspinnerpress.com

Contemporary Fantasy by ANDREW GREY

CPSIA information can be obtained at www.ICGtesting.com
Printed in the USA
LVOW110011080512

280668LV00003B/1/P